THE BLOOMINGSONS
OF THE
Nevada Sage

HALEY ROO

BY
Soozie Lewis

ISBN: 978-0-9827217-0-4

This book is a work of fiction. The names and characters are creations of the author's imagination except for the essence of the character of Buck, taken from a person who has been a great inspiration and help for the writing of this book. Any resemblance of characters other than Buck, or their names, to any actual persons living or dead is purely coincidental and unintentional!

Bible quotations have been taken from the King James Version.

Second Edition

NEVADA SAGE
P U B L I S H I N G

With love for our own pioneers, David, Crystal, and Grandma Raimondo.

A hearty thank you to Wendy Hoag for her enthusiastic encouragement for this book, and for the encouragement of my family.

A special thanks to my husband W. A. Lewis for all of his help and inspiration.

To see photographs of places mentioned in the book, go to the Author's Website: www.soozie-l.com.

Thanks Buck

Soozie Lewis

THE BLOOMINGSONS
OF THE NEVADA SAGE

– HALEY ROO! –

Illustrated by Wendy Hoag

Behold, what manner of love the Father hath bestowed upon us that we should be called the sons of God...

1 John 3:1a

Chapters

Storm!

"This is it?" My voice sounded creepy.

"Is this our house?" asked Roger. His voice reflected mine, with sounds of disappointment, dread and fascination all at the same time.

"This is the Bloomingson homestead, at least for now," said Dad.

"It's really out in nowhere isn't it?" said Mom.

We looked around us as if we had landed on a different planet. Not the kind that's devoid of life forms, but alive - a place of odd, scrubby sage plants and brown grass, with little things scurrying around on the ground, and Golden Eagles, Red-tailed Hawks and magpies overhead. They were birds we had never seen before. It was a strange place, so different than where we came from. The tame serenity of our country-suburban background had been suddenly broken. There was no ignoring it. In 1967, the hills of Nevada, and the Carson Valley below them that snuggled between the Sierra Nevada and Pine Nut Mountains, were still pretty much a wild place.

The small brown and beige farm house with a broken shutter and peeling paint, sat in lonely isolation in the middle of five acres, not too far from the base of Job's Peak. The front of it looked uninviting, like a face forlorn, and devoid of passion.

I lamented silently about our move, with a pouty frown that I hoped nobody else noticed. This wasn't how I had pictured things at all.

"Remember, we're just renting this until we can find a house to buy out here, pioneers," said Dad. He unlocked the door and we all went inside.

Our dog Ford, a brown and white Sheltie mix, who had little patience for waiting in the car with Sniffy our cat, even though Sniffy was still in his cage, ran in ahead of us. Ford was a good old guy, and I loved him, but he seemed to thunder in where even angels would have looked around the corner with caution. Sort of like my brother Roger. He ran in after Ford. They're just about on the same wavelength, I surmised quietly to myself. Monkey see, monkey do.

The inside of the house was very dark until Dad turned on the small chandelier made of discolored bronze that hung near the entryway.

"Is it - sort of an old farm house?" asked Mom.

"It's old alright!" said Roger. "Look. It's got one of those old black stoves in it." My nine-year-old brother was doing his usual nine-year-old evaluation of life, thinking he knew everything.

"A lot of the houses around here have these stoves in

them Roger," said Dad. "In fact, this one isn't very old. But it's not made too well." He frowned, as he looked it over.

"Aaaagghhhh! Oh no ...oh YUK!" I waved my hands in the air, almost slapping my own face. I ran over to Mom in little jumps, knocking into the side of her arm.

"Oh sorry Mom!" I couldn't help it!" Then I sort of wiggled all over. It was not my best display of coolness. Roger began to laugh.

"What's wrong Lissy!" said Mom.

"A spider! A spider! It's hanging from the ceiling! It almost went on my nose! Is it in my hair?"

"No, I don't see it on your head," said Mom. She looked at Dad. "Paul, will you get it for us please?"

"It felt like it hit my head!" It was trying to get on my nose! There were two other ones hanging by it too!" Everybody else seemed so calm. What did I have to do to convince everyone that I was almost attacked by one of the most wicked looking bugs in the universe! I could hardly believe that something so creepy could ever really happen!

Roger walked up and was staring closely at my head with buggy eyes. Like when you study a fly under a magnifying glass. "Does it have pointy feet?" he said. "The pointy feeted spiders are the ones that bite the hardest." He said that with no joke intended. "Bobby's friend Wade, told me that. And he knows a lot about spiders. But they don't scare ME!"

"Roger, just WAIT. One day a spider IS going to scare you!"

"They won't scare me," said Roger. "I like them."

I made sure he could see my disgusted frown.

"There he is," said Mom. "He's hanging right there. Oh look, there's the other two. I see them now. Eeouu!"

Dad waved his hand around and snatched the web, then threw the spider onto the ground and grabbed it with a kleenex. "Got him!" he said. He did the same with the other two, but one got away and scurried into a crack along the floorboard. "Okay. Let's hurry and bring our things in. It gets pretty cold around here after the sun goes down. Especially when it's almost winter like this."

"I'm already cold," I said, with a whine that sounded ten years younger than my official age of sixteen.

"Me too," said Mom. "Where's the heater switch, Hon."

"Uh...well," said Dad. "I tried to get the propane for our tank outside but the man can't come to do it for a few days. Something about their schedule...and their other driver is sick."

"No heat," said Mom bleakly.

"Well, not artificially," smiled Dad. "Don't worry, though, Katy my dear, be back in a minute. I'm off to chop wood. I made sure we had some here when I rented the house. There's food in the cupboards and refrig too. And look in the freezer."

It felt like it hit my head!

"Chop wood?" said Mom.

"Oh boy!" said Roger. "Can I help?"

"You can watch," called Dad as he went whistling out the door.

"Maaaammmmm," I moaned.

"Don't worry, Lissy. Dad will have a fire going in the stove in no time and we'll be snug as bugs in a rug." Then she saw my face with dread written all over it and said, "Well, never mind the bugs. Let's bring our things in."

Sure enough, there was a fire burning in the black stove before too long, but the heat didn't travel very far. We were all cold and tired and hungry. Mom and Dad made hamburgers in the kitchen. I opened a can of pork and beans and set the table with plastic silverware and paper plates.

Roger walked into the kitchen. "Look!" he said, "another spider," as he dangled it swinging from an almost invisible web. "They're all over the place! This one's from the front porch. And here's another one from the living room that I put in this jar!"

"Oh no," I cried. "I can't sleep here tonight!" The one thing in the physical world that bothered me the most, besides the thought of falling off a bridge, or getting caught in a fire, or being at a slumber party with a group of nasty girls that reveled in the distorted pleasures of a snotty click, was bugs! On me! No, I absolutely couldn't sleep here tonight!

"Yes you can, Lisbeth Bloomingson," said Dad. I

could tell he was tired from driving half a day to get here, and wasn't real patient with whiners. "After dinner we'll look around the house and clear out the bugs. Let's eat first. I'm starved."

"Roger," said Mom. She looked tired too. "Take your friends outside immediately, and don't invite them into the house again."

"Poor little guys. Come on Web, let's go," he said to the dangling spider.

"Boy is Roger getting weird out here," I complained.

"At least he's making the best of things," said Dad.

"That's true," said Mom. She looked a little strange when she said that. Did she agree with me? Or was she just too weary to think about it?

Before Roger left with his spider friends, Dad looked a little closer at them. "Roger," he said. "Don't play with the spiders anymore until I can look at them tomorrow with you in the daylight. The one in the jar is a young Black Widow. Take it outside carefully, away from the house and dump it. Don't let it get on you."

"Okay," said Roger very seriously. But he held it in the air like he prized it even more since it was now very 'dangerous.' My brother had a deranged priority list of what was fun, and so, even though he looked so 'seriously careful' walking that horrible bug out of the house, I could tell he was enjoying every minute of it. He couldn't fool me. I knew him.

When we were finished eating, I helped Mom clear

the table and Roger played with Sniffy on the kitchen floor. Sniffy's gray and black striped body twisted and turned while he chased a string that Roger dangled across his nose. Roger looked like he was having fun, but he sort of twisted and turned, almost like Sniffy in a funny sort of way. He stopped playing with Sniffy for a minute and stared. He dangled the string again, then rolled on the floor a little, stood up quickly and said, "Yikes!"

"What's wrong Roger?" said Mom.

"I've got to go," said Roger.

Mom and I stared at him standing there for a long time it seemed to me, for someone who had to "go."

Finally, Mom said, "Well okay then… go."

Roger just stood there making a miserable face. What was wrong with him!

"I don't want to," he said. Can I go outside?"

"Outside?" Mom and I both said it at the same time.

"Roger, we DON'T have an outhouse," I told him in disgust. "Even though it would really fit in with the atmosphere out here," I added quietly, reveling in my raunchy attitude.

"Why do you want to do that?" asked Mom.

"Because… the toilet is like an ice cube," said Roger.

It was true. Everything in the house became intensely cold after the sun went down. Especially metal, plastic, and porcelain. It actually hurt against our skin.

"Oh," said Mom. "That's right. It IS pretty cold. We'll see what we can do about it tomorrow. Tonight, just see if you can be a brave guy and rough it, okay?"

"Okay," he said. He walked like he wanted to get the torture over quickly, with his head down, towards the hall.

I had suffered through that revelation today myself. But I hadn't felt like talking about it and adding the 'toilet gripe' to my already long list of verbal woes. And what do you know, Mr. "Davy Crockett - King of the Wild Frontier – Spiderman," who enjoyed playing with repugnant bugs and would have scared me with them if he had been allowed to, couldn't handle the trauma of a frozen toilet just because it was as cold as an ice crag from the artic wasteland. Oh, would we all survive this move? Would I survive Roger?

The next day, the four of us drove around the valley, past ranches and farms and went to the Gardnerville grocery store. We bought more 'easy-fixins' food supplies and some bug killer. On the way back we drove down Muller Lane. Something – was in the road ahead. It looked like horses. There were also strange, low, moaning noises. Dad slowed the car down, while we all strained to hear out of our open windows, what was coming closer, and where. Suddenly in a clump, around the side of a ranch house, came a herd of cattle, all reddish brown with white faces, all trotting and crowded together. There were two cowboys, no, three, and as we got closer we could see that one of them was a boy not much older than Roger, on one of the horses. It was a short buckskin horse with quick moving legs. The boy was swinging a piece of rope over his head as he trotted along close to the cattle. He made a short wispy whistle directed at a calf out of line here, or a cow slowing up there. Roger's eyes were rippling with cowpoke delight as Mom looked back at him. Dad could see him in the rear view mirror.

"I think this valley has made a good impression on at least one of us so far," Dad said to Mom.

Roger had wanted a horse of his own, I think, before he was even born. He drove Mom and Dad nuts for the last two years that we lived in Walnut Creek, California. He wanted them to buy him a horse and board it for him somewhere. "No," they had said. "It's too far away for you to take care of it and feed it twice a day. "You'll just have to wait until we move someplace where we have enough property to keep a horse." Roger nagged and nagged and tried to coerce Mom and Dad into adopting an extremely old horse from a nice couple two streets away from us. They were moving, and Roger would have had to board the horse at another neighbor's house a half mile away. Dad put the kibosh on it before it turned into a real mess, but it left Roger with the horrible disappointment of the "I almose-hadda-horsa-my-own," trauma. And now, here we were in Nevada – with acres as far as we could see, until the mountains stopped them with their ragged border of green and brown pine trees.

While the cowpokes herded and the cows made their calm but complaining groans, Roger was sort of bouncing up and down in the car, like he was ready to jump out the window and swing up on the buckskin behind the miniature cowboy and whoop and whistle those cows on down the road.

His enthusiasm pretty much died out though, when we came home again to a very cold house. The fire had gone out. Dad had to chop some more wood. A hungry Ford and Sniffy had to be fed. That night we all huddled down into our covers and tried to be happy with food and shelter, and the prospect of possibly warming up our feet if we laid still and didn't kick the extra afghans laying across our legs onto the floor.

Roger and I were in our beds in a small room outside Mom and Dad's. Mine was a double and his was a twin. That's about all the furniture we had in our room, except for a little lamp sitting on the floor in the corner. We weren't going to unpack most of our things that the movers had brought until we moved to our final home, so it was sort of like camping. It was creepy here at night in a strange place, in the blackness with no streetlights, or even lights from a distant city. I was actually glad to be in a room with my little brother, even though I would never tell anybody that and thought that I probably needed my brain analyzed.

Things were finally quiet so I could think about – what were we doing out here! I was remembering how Roger and I felt when we had found out about our sudden move. Dad's company had expanded and his job shifted from representing the latest in car accessories, to farm and ranching equipment. We had to move so quickly from Walnut Creek that we even missed the Walnut Festival, which came once a year at the end of September. Roger and I were in the deep blue sea of doldrums when we had to leave our contented little suburban town, and the kids that we knew, and wouldn't be able to gorge ourselves on corndogs, sno-cones and cotton candy at the Walnut Festival. No Rock-O-Plane, no ring toss, no helium balloons, no nothing. And we came out to this?

I was laying there in the dark, unable to see anything at all, even with my eyes wide open. I was glad Dad was going to buy some night-lights at the hardware store tomorrow. Because of the total darkness, I started to picture things more easily from Walnut Creek. I thought about Jeff Crenshaw, a friendly guy that my friend Joy and I would eat lunch with out on the lawn at school. I knew that he liked me a lot and I liked him. He had been a nice enough guy, but sort of like a big kid or something. I thought of Gregory Harper who sat in my sophomore biology class in front of me and to the right. He had moved to our town the last year and made a pretty big popularity splash as soon as he got there. He was one of the coolest guys in our school - according to a lot of girls who claimed to have gone out with him, or "almost gone out with him," or had "had a really good time talking with him." He did have that sex appeal and charisma that not a lot of high school guys have in such abundance. I hadn't ever had a real conversation with him. I only said, "Thanks," when I dropped my pencil one day and he picked it up for me when it had rolled under his chair. I don't know why I liked him so much after just looking at the back of his head for six months. I just did. How silly. Just like all the other stupid girls that admired him and stared at him like a drove of drooling female cattle. The realization that I would never get to know him better and really talk to him, although the thought of that made me nervous, and that I wouldn't be there to study the way his hair made little swirls at the back of his neck, made me fall farther into the mud bog of 'poor me.' There would never be anybody that I ever felt that way about again. Especially in Nevada.

For a minute I listened to Roger making little nasally noises in between breathing, so I figured he was asleep. Then, surprisingly, I fell asleep too.

At about two o'clock in the morning a fierce howling wind began to whirl its way through the valley and it seemed to gather around the lonely drafty house and whip its way up under the eaves. It went through the cracks, around the windows, and then CRASH! With a mighty roar it slammed against the side of the house by Mom and Dad's room. It did this three times until everyone in the house was wide-awake. Before long, Mom and Dad heard two pairs of anxious feet coming into the large bedroom, and at the fourth crash, our two pairs of feet jumped into the bed on top of Dad's legs and then buried themselves in the covers.

"It's only wind," said Dad. "I've heard it can blow pretty good out here in the valley, but I didn't know it would be quite like this..."

"WHOOOOSHHHH! CLAPPP! CRASH!" The wind was having a field day with our lonesome homestead, like a playground bully finding a solitary victim to pound on. The broken shutter banged loudly in a disjointed rhythm against the front of the house.

"Mom, I'm scared!" Roger cried.

"I don't like it either," I said. "Why did we move out here to this terrible place?"

"I want to go home," said Roger.

"Now everybody listen to me," said Dad. "I know how you feel. I don't like to be cold either. And it gets dark out here very early because of the mountains blocking the sun. I know that it's no fun to have most of your things packed away in boxes, and this wind IS a nuisance, but we still have a lot of things to be thankful for. We have plenty of food, we have warm blankets, and we have each other! We're just staying here until we can find our new home. The wind is noisy but it won't hurt us. Remember how we've talked about God still being with us through the storm? Well, this is a kind of storm. A storm of difficulty. But we need to persevere."

"How can we persevere?" asked Roger. "What do we do?"

"The first thing we do," said Dad, "is to trust God.

Throw worry out the window and let the wind carry it away. I really believe that God has led us out here. Good times will come. Hey, remember when God led Moses and the Israelites to the Promised Land?"

"I don't want to be like Moses and the Israelites," said Roger in a teeny little voice. "I want to go home!"

I could see Roger's face in the moonlight coming through the window. He looked like a little pug dog with an upset stomach.

Mom put her arm around Roger and gave him a big hug. "This is our new home," she said softly.

Then Dad prayed with us. That was something that we usually did around the dinner table, thanking God for our food, and making prayer requests. Tonight, we needed some extra emergency praying - that we would be safe, and could somehow appreciate the place that we were at now. "Okay pioneers," he said suddenly, after closing the prayer. "I have an idea. Let's all get up for awhile."

"Now?" said Roger. "Oh boy! I get to be up in the middle of the night!" Then he fell off the bed and landed on the floor with a loud "clump!" sound.

"Are you okay, Roger!" asked Mom.

We heard him roll around for a minute then saw him pop his head up at the foot of the bed.

"I'm okay!" he said. Roger was such a dufus sometimes, but I didn't say anything. I thought maybe we should stick together right then. I couldn't exactly explain why.

We all got up and put on our bathrobes and went down to the small living room at the other end of the house that had the very inefficient black stove. Mom and I made hot chocolate and we all sat down at the foot of the "better than nothing" hearth. There was still a fierce monster of a wind, driven like a steam engine, along the foot of the mountains near us. When it quieted down between gusts, we could hear a terrible forlorn howling and then a frenzied yipping in the distance.

"What was that?" I said.

"I think it's coyotes," said Dad. They're a ways away, though." He looked sleepy and thoughtful, but not bothered.

Then we heard some closer sounds. What were they? How strange. It was hard to tell, as the increasing decibels were distorted by the wind.

Roger and I looked out the window, blocking the light from inside the house with our hands. Dad turned the light overhead down low, then he turned the table lamp off. He put his head close to the glass too, and looked out the window. The small, outside porch light was still on. It was dim, and broken around the metal base, but it was enough to reflect evidence that the owners of the monstrous noises that we were hearing were in our own backyard! In the dark we saw little lights. Little tiny yellowish lights that moved a little. Then stopped. I counted seven. No, there were eight. Some of the lights changed color a little. They seemed to move closer towards the house. A phantom scream sliced the air. Then a long howl. Then another one. Then a yipping in a sort of singing fashion. Then the yipping turned frenzied. Dad turned on a brighter spotlight that sat in the shadows next to the dim porch light. We could finally see enough to catch sight of the eyes' owners. Two of them were pulling at a tan colored animal body. The other two were looking over at the house. Could they see our faces in the window? Probably. One coyote dropped his end of the kill, and the other one trotted off into the bushes with it. The rest followed.

Roger and I stood with our heads leaning on the window as if our bangs were glued to the glass.

"Coyotes," said Dad. "That must have been a huge jack rabbit that they got."

Roger looked at Dad, then at me. He didn't say anything. Right then, I don't think he was able to talk.

Dad turned the table lamp back on. A sudden gust of wind swirled around outside of the house, then became a roar, before it beat against the large sliding glass door without warning in the room where we were sitting. The door was hit so hard, that it bowed under the strength of the wind, and opened up the bottom part under the glass frame. A blast of wet, icy particles combined with dust, had blown under the bowed glass door into the house.

"What is that!" we all said.

"I never thought I'd see something like that," said Dad. "It looks like a snow flurry. Looks like it bent the door and blew itself right into the house!"

"What a strange night," said Mom.

"Wow, that's kind of spooky," said Roger. "It's almost like a monster or something." Roger looked like he was watching a horror movie, only without the enjoyment and the popcorn. Mom and Dad didn't let Roger see the really awful movies, but he did know how scary things could be. I think humans know in their guts that danger and evil really exist, even when they're young.

"It's just the wind," said Dad. Then he said to Mom, "The worst monster, is demoralization."

"I know," she said, while getting up to look out of the window herself.

"What's a demoralization monster?" asked Roger. I was surprised he could catch that whole word so well. He must have been in his top form for paying attention. Right now, he was probably afraid not to.

I said to him, "That's when you let everything scare you into… " I stopped to think. "…into, nothing."

"Into nothing?" he said.

"Yes," I said. "Fear stops you, and keeps you from doing things right, and turns you into nothing, sort of. But because of God, we don't have to be nothing… " I looked at Dad.

"Methinks we have a great theologian!" said Dad. He gave me a hug and said, "I couldn't have said it better myself, Lissy Girl!" I always liked it when he called me Lissy Girl. Just the way he said it sounded like, "I love you and think you're swell."

"We don't need to be afraid, Roger," I said. Wow, I sounded so different than I did the first night we had got here. It was so creepy tonight that I HAD to depend on God!

"That's right, Roger," said Dad. "And remember, animals have to eat too. All those coyotes were doing out there, was getting dinner."

"That's right," said Mom. "Could you imagine them criticizing us for having a barbecue?"

Roger still looked a little sheepish and sat on the couch arm next to Mom. He smiled a little. Sometimes Mom could be funny.

"But I don't like animals dying," he said.

"Neither do I," said Dad. "But one day it won't be that way."

"Aren't you glad that Ford doesn't want to eat Sniffy?" I said, lifting my eyebrows and smiling at Roger. "He's too bratty for anybody to eat anyways, and he has stinky cat food breath." I didn't want Roger to feel bad about the 'dog eat dog' world of nature. I also didn't want to feel too bad about it myself.

Roger giggled a little at my silliness.

We started laughing and talking, and drank some more hot chocolate. I could tell that we all felt better, like we had faced the difficulties and said, "but we'll make it." I think Mom and Dad felt a little better because I had talked like we would make it, even though I hadn't lived it out yet, and was still a little uneasy about a lot of things.

The wind had died down, but the distant howling continued as Dad walked with us back to our beds in the cold little room. I felt kind of silly and chicken-livered again, even at sixteen, and was glad that Dad stayed with us until we got into bed. But I had good reason, I logically convinced myself. I could already see that even with our modern conveniences, to be a REAL Nevadan, meant a hard rift for my brother Roger and I, with some of the old comforts of the Bay Area. We were freezing our tail feathers off in a lonely wilderness land, dodging crawling creatures that hung in every room of the house and listening to scary noises in the night, while our friends and neighbors were back in Walnut Creek, riding the Ferris Wheel and the Scrambler and winning stuffed monkeys and chocolate cakes by throwing clothespins into milk bottles in 78 degree weather.

Roger and I listened to the howling for a while, and then to our surprise we began to feel sleepy.

"We'll be okay, Roger Muskrat." It's the word I used to tease him, and let him know that I thought he was 'okay' and he seemed to like it.

"I know." He said.

We didn't talk any more until we fell asleep.

2

Snow Palace

The morning slipped in behind the night with the most peaceful silence. As Roger and I tossed in our beds from the light sneaking in around our window shade, Dad walked through our room.

"Are you awake yet pioneers?"

We both looked at him with droopy eyes. I sat up in bed, while Roger turned over onto his side and pulled the sheet across his face.

"Is it time to get up yet?" I asked.

"It sure is. It's almost nine o'clock." Then he said, "Look out your window."

Roger groaned as I lifted up the shade.

"It's...it's all white...What is it Dad? Is it snow?"

"It's snow all right. It must be a special snow. It's very early this year."

"Snow?" Roger flipped up on top of his covers and was over to the window as quick as a light beam. "It IS snow! It's snow! Oh boy, oh boy!" "Dad, can we go out and play in it?" he begged, with sleepy eyes that became more excited the longer he looked out the window.

"Sure. Get your jackets and boots on."

"Oh boy, oh boy," Roger was saying again. "I've never even seen snow before. Now I get to play in it!"

I didn't want to act too excited about going out and PLAYING with Roger, because it seemed sort of juvenile, but who is even out here, I thought, to see me or even care about me doing anything uncool! I got dressed in the bathroom and was back in the bedroom getting my shoes on, even before he was ready. I had never been in snow before either, or got to touch it or see it falling, except in movies or on Christmas cards.

There were acres and acres surrounding our house with a large front yard fenced with split logs. Everything was white except for the sides of the fence rails. We were in a world of pure, clean brightness and rich wooden browns. Every limb of the four cottonwood trees near the house had a layer of fluffy snow on it.

The sun peeked out off and on through the snowy mist. As we walked and twirled and slipped around outside, we noticed that every twig of every weed, every blade of the growing things in the fields that were touched by the sun's rays, were covered with beautiful gleaming crystals. We were in a sparkling snow palace. I knew that Roger and I would remember this day forever.

We played and laughed and ran while Mom and Dad watched us through the window, until we were out of breath and very hungry. Mom reminded us to stomp the snow off of our boots before coming in. We came in smiling, with flakes of white on our hair, and red noses, telling Mom and Dad about the strange and wonderful feeling of being surrounded with white in a silent world of peaceful, falling flakes.

"I know," said Dad. "It's wonderful isn't it! Time for breakfast."

As we were sitting down at the table, I looked out the window. "It's just as if God had taken a handful of snowflakes and sprinkled them on every plant and weed, just so evenly. Just so perfectly," I said.

Roger had his nose pressed against the window. "Yeah!" he said. Not a great communication maneuver, but the spirit was there, and breakfast that morning was one of the nicest that our family ever had.

After breakfast we went outside again, to the snow. Ford and Sniffy followed us out to one of the irrigation ditches behind the house. The water in it was frozen so solid that Roger and I could walk on it. It was less than two feet deep, so we took off skating down the length of it in our snow boots. Sniffy stayed on the bank, but Ford was having so much fun running around with us that day, that he jumped onto the ice with his four feet splaying out in all different directions.

"Look Lissy," said Roger. "He's just like Bambi!" We had seen 'Bambi' on T.V. right before we moved. Ford did look pretty silly, but really happy, and slipped and skidded across the ice to the other bank, then ran up to the grassy weeds and dirt, turned around, and looked at us, barking, like he thought that he had just done something wonderful.

"Does he know how stupid he looks?" said Roger, laughing. "I wonder if I look that stupid sometimes," he said, more thinking out loud, than talking to me.

I didn't say anything. I didn't want to get us crabby and fighting because we were having such a good time.

"Lissy, he said to me, "what do we do when it's all gone?"

"When what's all gone?"

"The snow. We haven't had this much fun since we've been here. What will we do when the snow's gone?"

"We'll have fun doing something else," I said. Was I telling HIM that, or myself?

"But what will we do?"

"I don't know. We can't see the future. Only God can."

"But if I can't see the future, how will I know what to do in it?"

"I think that's what faith is," I said. "Faith in God, I mean."

"Oh," said Roger. "I think I'm gonna faith some more snow."

"That sounds good to me," I said. I threw a loose little ball of snow towards his freckled cheek. His light red hair looked grayish tan in the shadow of the snow clouds. He shook the snow off of his bangs and face and smiled a big grin with one missing tooth.

We'll do fine out here. We'll make it, I thought. We've just got to.

3

Mystery of Romance

Two weeks later Mom had some good news for Roger and I as we came into the house after school. My friend Joy and her younger brother Bobby were coming to see us. We were thrilled! There was absolutely nobody at all near our house to do things with and we still hadn't made any real friends with anybody at our new schools in the valley. Joy and Bobby were coming Saturday, with their parents. I really missed Joy and was glad to have her friendship out here, even if it was only for one weekend, but I was also glad about something else. I could find out a little something maybe, about Gregory Harper. What was going on back 'home' with him, and which of the one hundred and fifty other girls at school that were interested in him, were involved? Just how much, I wondered, was I missing?

The day finally came. I had put on my new black jeans with a pink shirt. I wanted to look a little spiffy for today. Roger just put on some of the same old clothes that he would wear every day to play in - his washed out green shirt with the little brown moccasins and teepees on them, and blue faded jeans - and seemed contented that he was perfectly dudded up for the occasion.

The Leftland family car was coming up the driveway. There were still patches of snow on the ground from the snowfall that had come about every three days for the last two weeks. It was an unusually heavy snow fall in the valley for the beginning of October. The Sierra mountains behind our house were a fantastic display of white and dark green, traveling up and down the west side of the valley, with the more serenely shaped rolling Pine Nut mountains in their angelic blanket of white on the east side.

"Katy," Mrs. Leftland yelled to Mom from the car. "It's absolutely gorgeous out here!"

"Hi Lissy!" called Joy.

"Bobby! Bobby!" Roger almost climbed into the car before they could grab their coats and hats and open the door all the way to get out.

"Hi Roger!" said Mr. Leftland. "How are you doing Paul?" He reached out to shake hands with Dad.

"Just fine," said Dad.

"This is really a great place to be," said Mr. Leftland as he took in a big breath of the clear crispy air.

"How are things going for all of you back in Alamo?" asked Dad.

Alamo was an even smaller town next door to Walnut Creek. Joy's family lived right on the edge of it, so she went to the same high school that I did. Sometimes

Joy and I would ride our bikes back and forth from our houses along the small Alamo highway that was canopied overhead with huge golden leafed trees.

"Oh we're doing just fine there," said Mr. Leftland, "in spite of the continuous building. We're going to be losing more open space according to what I've been reading in the papers. Orchards are going to be a thing of the past before long," he said, shaking his head. "We miss all of you, too... Sure glad we could make it out here!" he said, brightening a little. " How about a look around?"

"Great," said Dad.

Joy and I walked off together over by the little wooden shed at the left of the house and sat down on two large tree stumps.

"Your hair's already getting longer!" said Joy. It looks really cute in braids."

I pulled on one of my dark blond braids with my hand. "You really think so? I don't know what else to do with it but braid it, right now. It just gets in a big mess out here if I don't."

"Yeah, I like it" she said. "I like your pink shirt too. It goes good with your brown eyes. Wait a minute." She looked closer. "They're actually green with brown in them, aren't they? I never noticed that before."

"Yeah, I guess so. Thanks," I said. That's one thing that I missed about not being around Joy. She wasn't the jealous type, and not afraid to give you a compliment from time to time. She also had been the sort of unofficial 'fashion consultant' for a lot of us girls at school.

"Well what's going on back at our old stomping grounds of higher learning?" I asked about my old school, thinking of Gregory and feeling a little left out because Joy was there and I wasn't.

"Oh, not a whole lot… Mr. Shaheen got married."

"No!" I said.

Joy shook her head yes. Her long red ponytail bounced and her blue eyes flickered with delight when she added, "And guess who he married! Miss Williams!"

"No!" I said again. "You're kidding!"

"No! I'm not!" she said laughing.

"Why didn't we know about this?" I said with irritation. "A romance going on right under our noses and we didn't even know it!"

"Really!" said Joy. "We could have been enjoying the whole thing for who knows how long!"

We sat there for a minute picturing those two pretty reserved high school teachers coming closer together than just having coffee in the teachers' lounge, and pondering on how surprising the mystery of romance can be, when I asked Joy, "Well what's going on with the kids that we know?" Really, Joy, I thought to myself, don't you get it? Gregory Harper. Gregory Harper!

"Oh I don't know," she said… "Carol Barns had her appendix out. She was sort of in the danger zone for a while, but she's okay now. Actually, she was in more of a danger zone from the "shag" haircut that she got, right before her surgery. It was awful. They cut it way too short and her ears stuck out. It was more like a "bubble" and those are definitely on the way out. I think she had been in more agony from that, than her appendix. I was thinking of getting a shag, but I think I'll just get a trim and wear a flip. But Carol recovered from both things." Joy nodded her head up and down for a minute as if to confirm to herself that Carol was okay. "Why, who else were you thinking of?" Joy gave a sly little smile.

Okay, so she's going to torture and shame me at the same time. "Oh," I said, trying to be so smooth and look only halfway caring, "people like... maybe Gregory Harper?"

"Ohhhhhh... " Joy said, looking at me with slanty eyes. "Gregory... " she said with her best Victorian style accent, then continued, "Yes, well, old Gregory, that idiot!"

"What do you mean?" I said with incredulous disbelief, since I knew for a fact that she, and a number of other girls in our school, had the same sort of 'interest' in Gregory, that I had.

"He got in trouble at school for letting the air out of Mr. Wendelman's tires, and the vice-principal's too. They suspended him for three days. He made both of the principals late for Superintendent meetings. But I think they were REALLY mad at him, mostly, because Mr. Wendelman was in such a hurry that day and ran out to his car while he was still cleaning his glasses, and he got inside the car and drove off a ways, before he realized that he was bumping around on his rims.

Jim Treller saw the whole thing."

"Oh," I said, still trying to picture Gregory doing something so nervy.

"Gregory", said Joy, with her Victorian accent again, "was already on the bad side of Mr. Wendelman after throwing up in the cafeteria."

"What?" I said, horror stricken.

Joy shook her head up and down again with her red tail bouncing. "He threw up on Rebecca Wainwright's PURSE! It splashed on her new mohair sweater and she really gave him heck for that! He couldn't have picked a worse person to throw up on. She's always been such a little snip. Sometimes I think he did it on purpose. But maybe not. That's pretty radical. I could see him burping in her face maybe... "

While Joy babbled on I sat there in shock. The White Knight of my own personal mental diary had just done some of the worst faux pas for our high school society. How could he be so icky? I don't know which thing turned me off the most, the vandalism to the cars, or throwing up in public on a crabby girl that everyone had a hard time dealing with even when barf wasn't in the picture. Maybe, I decided, I will reserve my fondest affections in the future, until I get to see more of how a person operates.

"... and so, he's just in the doghouse for now," Joy continued. She was quiet for a minute, then she said, looking around at our yard and the mountains, "Wow, you know Lissy, it's really neat out here."

Roger and Bobby came bumbling on by us, kicking ice-encrusted twigs around, eating snow and spitting it into the air, and then finally, making snowballs and throwing it at us. Yes, this was just like it had been back in Walnut Creek with our two brothers, Joy and I both agreed.

We had a great time with our good friends. They spent Saturday night at our house and went to church with us in the morning. They had to leave Sunday afternoon when dinner was over. It was hard for us to see them go.

"We'll come back again," said Joy. "Mom and Dad said that we will."

"I know," I said. But I was pretty sad. I was thinking again how I still hadn't made any real new friends at school yet, out here, in our new home away from home.

It didn't really hit Roger that they would be leaving until Bobby was putting on his jacket and gathering up the toy cars that he had brought for Roger to see and play with. He handed one of them out of the car window to Roger and said, "Here, you keep this one."

It was hard to look normal when we were all waving goodbye, even for Mom and Dad. Everyone was quiet when we went into the house.

Roger was almost crying. "There's nothing to do here when our friends go home."

Dad lifted Roger into the air and said, "In about a week we're going to be busier than ever. Mom and I have found us a house earlier than we expected. Remember last week when we went with Mrs. Fairwell from church to look at houses, while you and Lissy walked around Genoa and went to the park and museum? Well, we're buying one of the houses that we liked the best. We just got a telephone call this morning from our realtor. The people who are selling the house accepted our offer."

Roger's mouth was hanging open a little bit, and my eyes were glued to Dad as he went on. "It's out in a warmer place where the sun shines longer. We'll still have Jackrabbits, cottontails, eagles and hawks, and coyotes out there, but in the evenings, I've been told, wild horses come down out of the Pine Nut mountains, and walk through the undeveloped land between houses to graze in those huge open spaces along the road."

"Wild horses..." said Roger almost breathlessly.

I looked at Dad in awe. "Really?"

"That's right."

"We're really going to live out there?" I asked.

"Yes, we are. And since the house has four acres of land with it, the Lord willing, we can have horses out there, of our own."

"We can?" said Roger. "We can?" He was in a little bit of a daze and didn't really pay attention to the rest of what Dad, Mom and I were talking about while he plopped onto a chair in the living room.

Later, when I went back out into the yard with Roger, he was quiet and looked at me with, I can only describe it as, an older and wiser look.

"Well, what's going on in YOUR little brain today, Roger Muskrat," I said, teasing him.

He said, while looking up at the sky, "God's really up there isn't he."

"Yes," I said, taking the opportunity to look older and wiser myself, "In fact, he's everywhere."

"So he knows what's going on all the time with us."

"Oh yeah," I said.

"So it WAS better for me to wait for the right time to have a horse – instead of getting that real old boney horse of the neighbor's and letting him live a long ways away from us."

"Oh yeah," I said again, nodding my head.

Roger looked back up into the clear Nevada sky. He sure was quiet. It must have been a really sacred moment in the life of my usually squirrelly, annoying, and maker of gross noises, little brother. In fact, I think he might have even been praying, but I didn't want to ask him. At least, not right then, I thought.

4

Wilderness Haven

"Just look at those stars," said Mom. "They just sparkle and twinkle so brightly that you want to reach right up in the sky and pick one out and hold it in your hand like a firefly..."

" I know what you mean," said Dad. "We didn't see the stars like this where we came from. I've never seen a sky so clear as this."

"But Mom," Roger said from inside, through the open screened window of our new home, "the stars are too hot to hold in your hand, and they're too far away, and they're so big! A lot bigger than a firefly..."

"Boy Roger, you sure don't understand things sometimes," I said, standing next to Mom and Dad outside. "Mom knows all of those facts! She's just being romantic."

"Romantic?" said Roger peering into the dark. "Romantic?" He said it with the kind of tone that he had used once, when telling about a spider that had eaten, while stuck in its web, a littler spider of almost the same color...

"Romantic out here?" continued Roger. " Kissing and hugging and stuff? You said this was cowboy land. I bet cowboys never did that stuff."

"Not that kind of romantic," said Mom. "I mean jackrabbit romantic and wild horse romantic..."

"And star romantic," I added, feeling a little older than my usual self, since I understood all this and he didn't.

It was truly a beautiful place for those who opened their eyes to the value of the living dessert. It was alive with wildlife, insects, and sagebrush of different kinds. There were even wildflowers that bloomed from out of the earth where no hose had ever lain, or watering can had ever sprinkled. There were a few young trees in the area, planted here and there by homeowners and some scattered clumps of older trees, mostly Poplar and Aspen, but it was amazing how well the trees that were out there grew and flourished. The rich sandy soil was perfect for growing things, especially potatoes and other vegetables. Flowers and rosebushes did well too. All of these things flourished when given plenty of water in the warm dry land.

We were settling well into our new house across the Carson Valley, at the foot of the Pine Nut Mountains. Our house faced north, but looking out the back south window to the west we could see the towering Sierra Nevada Mountains. They seemed even more spectacular from a distance than they did close up. They were patchy with snow and brownish green colors. The spots where there were few trees between the massive dark green areas gave the appearance of huge veins running in a crooked course down the sides of the steep towering peaks. The very top of the mountain profile running the whole length of the valley looked like it had been drawn by an artist's hand with pen and ink - one fine, perfect line, dividing mountains and sky, with not a blur to mar the exquisite beauty and grace of the heaven-molded earth.

The winter had been unusually short but with extremely cold winds and heavy snowfall. Our family had fared better in our warmer house here across the valley where the sun shines longer and the air is even dryer than it was on the west side. The chilling winter mist that hung snugly around the mountains where we had first lived was no longer a problem.

Christmas had come and gone with much gladness and celebration. There were visits from relatives, snowball fights, and even a sleigh ride up at Lake Tahoe, with red bell straps jingling to the jolting trots of the huge honey brown Belgian horses.

It was technically winter in February, but an early spring was making its way into the valley this year, and with it, newborn lambs and calves, colts and fillies of every color, and a warm green blanket was replacing the brown snow-burned pastures of the winter. The sagebrush and Russian thistle were coming alive with color. Yellows, pinks and purples. The delicate blossoms on the scattered plants would do justice to the most cultivated gardens in the world. We were learning to appreciate things other than buying caramel corn at the shopping mall, toy stores for Roger, clothes stores for me, television, and carnivals. And although we wouldn't turn up our noses at any one of those things, we were realizing a different way of life, and the unspoiled beauty of a wilderness land.

Now on this pleasant evening, we were enjoying God's creation all over again as we had done so many times before.

"What's that noise?" said Roger with his nose pressed against the screen.

"What noise?" I said.

"Shhhh!" said Dad. "I think I hear it Rog."

"What!" I whispered. "What!"

"Shhh...sort of a clomping noise and some rustling. It's coming from our back pasture. Turn the lights off."

We were quiet for a minute.

"Oh I hear it now," I said.

"So do I," said Mom. "And I think I know what it is. It must be the horses."

"You mean the wild horses?" I asked.

"Yes, Sam Newman told me that the mustangs have been traveling through the yards two streets down from here and grazing out by the road going to the highway."

Mr. Newman was our next-door neighbor, who lived

on the property to the right of us on the west side.

"Remember the little herd that we saw two days ago? Well that must be them coming through now."

"Really Mom?" said Roger. "That's really them? Wow!"

We all remembered the thrill of seeing the small herd of nine horses and four foals in the grassy land along the road. Mares looking up now and then from their grazing to study cars and their noises that came close to them while stopped alongside the shoulder. The horses looked back into our staring smiling faces inside the car windows. One foal had been laying down, another one sleeping. Two of the larger foals ran through the sagebrush in stiff-legged little lopes around one large brown horse, then back, then stopping to look and sniff the air. It had been a delightful sight to behold, under a glistening yellow sun in the ice blue sky.

"Listen," said Dad from out of the dark again. "You can hear them nickering."

"I wonder if they're talking to each other," I said.

"It might be the stallion telling the mares to follow him," said Roger. "In a quiet sort of way, of course."

"A lot of times it's an older mare that leads the group of horses. But I guess it could be a stallion," said Dad. I could almost hear a smile on his face. He was enjoying the romance of the evening too, but we couldn't see him or each other very well because it was dark and the only light around us came from the bright stars overhead.

"Well, time for bed Roger," said Mom.

"Ohhhh..." Roger moaned. " Not yet Mom! Not yet! Not now."

"Yes, now! There will be plenty of times to see and hear the horses. They've been living out here longer than we have, you know."

"Aw, Mom," said a droopy Roger as he walked slowly in front of her through the dining room. "Sometimes I don't think I'll ever really get a horse. We've been in Nevada for over four months! I heard you tell a lady at church that, like you thought it was a long time! I'm tired of waiting!"

"Roger, you know that we need to finish our fence off and make some repairs on it. We would like to have a cushion of money for vet bills and unexpected things that a horse might need. Be patient. Now go brush your teeth."

We were in the bathroom together brushing our teeth at the large double sinks. I usually waited to brush alone, about an hour or so after Roger went to bed, but I was tired tonight and just wanted to get it over with and turn in early.

"Sometimes it's hardest to be patient," said Roger, "right when you think your prayer is about to be answered, or at least, when you think it SHOULD be answered. I just don't think I can wait any longer. I just can't." He squished the toothpaste tube in the middle with his fist and squeezed a large hunk of green toothpaste onto his brush, much more than he should have, and brushed his teeth very hard with angry looking eyes. Then after he rinsed his mouth we heard Mom and Dad talking as they walked by the door on the way to their bedroom.

"They said that Will is doing very well under the circumstances," Dad was telling Mom. "The plane that his father was in, crashed on Job's Peak. On that desolate crag, it'll take longer than he thought for the rescue team to get the bodies out. They had to set the funeral for next week. Will said that he couldn't hardly stand the thought of waiting to get that over with but that he called on the Lord to help him to be patient."

Will was a nineteen-year-old boy that Roger had met once where Dad worked.

Roger was done rinsing his mouth. He looked at himself in the mirror. His cheeks were a little red. "I feel bad for Will," he whispered to me. "I guess I can wait a little while longer to get a horse."

I felt a little shaky too after hearing about Will. "I know what you mean," I said to Roger. "I'm going to try to be more patient about meeting people and having interesting things happen."

Roger picked up the toothpaste tube and straightened it out as good as he could, then put the cap back on before he put it on the cabinet shelf behind the mirrored door.

5

Buck MacCleod

Sometimes things happen suddenly. Especially when a person has said, I'll wait, God. I SHOULD wait, so I will. That suddenness is sometimes like a bug hitting a windshield, or like a bird darting from a tree past your window to your rooftop. Or sometimes it's like a sprinkler turning on all of a sudden when you're standing in the way of it, and before you can turn around, or crack a knuckle or say boo, you're all wet. That's sort of what happened to Roger and I on that early spring-like day. In fact, it was an almost cold Tuesday, since the weather had been going back and forth from warm and pleasant to gusty and cooler, at four-thirty in the evening, under a dry clear sky when Roger walked around the side of our house to carry a piece of wood from Dad's truck. As he set it on the stack in the back of the house, he caught for an instance from the side of his eye, the outline of a small brown and white horse in the far end of our property where the sagebrush grew full and high. He looked up and stared.

The little horse had heard the sound of the wood being dropped and he had looked up also. The two of them stood looking at each other until the horse took a few steps and sniffed the air. Then he turned around and went slowly towards the back opening of our south acres where two sections of the fence were missing and the gate was down.

Roger could hardly tell his feet which way to go. I could hear him calling around the side of the house, then he changed direction and went through the back door.

"Dad! Dad! Oh Lissy!" he said as he bumped into me in the doorway. "Where's Dad? Where's Mom?"

"In the front yard. Why?"

"There's a horse. A horse in our back yard. And he's real pretty! You should see him!"

Roger and I ran to the front yard and Mom and Dad followed us quickly into the back. The little horse was gone.

"Ohhhhh..." said Roger, "He's not here now. He went out the back gate. Ohhhh...I wish you could have seen him."

"I saw him," said a voice from the back yard next door.

Roger looked over towards Mr. Newman's house. I followed the direction of his nose and saw a young guy in a brown cowboy hat standing there with his hand leaning on one of Mr. Newman's poplar trees.

"The little Paint." the guy said. "Looks like he's been

running with that herd that stays down at the old sod farm."

"The herd?" Roger said. "You mean the wild horse herd?"

"Sure thing," he said back to Roger, glancing at Dad and I at the same time. "They've been coming through our back pastures at night."

"We've heard them making a little noise when it's been dark out there," said Dad to the guy. He went over to shake his hand. "Hi there. I'm Paul Bloomingson. This is my wife Katy and my daughter Lissy, and son Roger. Are you any relation to Mr. Newman?"

"I'm his grandson." He stood straight and tall, at least to me, but he was actually of medium height, and shook Dad's hand with confidence even though I thought he hid a little look of shyness. It made me look at the ground for a minute, before I had the nerve to look up again at him and study his tanned face with the serious but boyish look framed by his soft brown hair and golden brown eyes.

"I'm Whether Alvie MacCleod. But Grandpa and my other relatives call me 'Buck'."

Buck was seventeen years old, and definitely my senior in more than just age. He didn't have that "cool" sort of air about him, but seemed, well, sort of grown-up. He had a blue plaid shirt on with a denim jacket. The bottom of his Levis covered his feet except for the tip of his black cowboy boots. He looked friendly, with a soft but genuine smile. Before my mind could even register everything, I felt an unmistakable sensation. The summation of everything I had learned or saw, or decided on during the whole of my years on earth, told me without question, that this was a person of substance, and that I liked him. Now how could that be, I wondered. I felt uncomfortable, like everybody could see right through my forehead into my brain.

Dad seemed to warm up to Buck right away after talking to him for a few minutes until Mr. Newman called Buck from his barn next door and asked him to come and help him move something heavy. Dad said we'd see him later if he would still be there when Mr. Newman came over that evening.

"Sure thing," he said back. "Nice meeting you." He smiled and nodded to Dad and Mom, but glanced at me before he turned to go. I watched him walk away.

Roger looked after him for a minute too, then asked me quietly, "Is he a cowboy?"

"He looks like one," I said quietly back to him.

"Wow!" said Roger. "A real cowboy."

That night Mr. Newman came over, and he brought Buck along with him. Buck was spending some time with Mr. Newman and helping him mend his fence in some places and put new shingles on his roof. They came for pie and coffee. Roger told Buck and Mr. Newman about the horse in our back pasture and how it didn't seem to be afraid and didn't run off, but walked away.

"Hmmmm," said Mr. Newman as he chewed softly on a bite of lemon meringue pie. "The wild horses

He stood straight and tall, at least to me...

around here don't usually run unless someone gets close to them. But I'm surprised that he would separate from the herd like that. And around here, the wild horses that I've seen are usually solid colors too. Did you see him about four o'clock?"

"It was about four-thirty," said Dad.

"Yep. That's about the right time," said Mr. Newman. "It's unusually early for the horses to pass through here but I did see a small herd go between the property lines in the back at about three-thirty this afternoon. He must have had a hankering to just stop and eat. And you do have some grass on your land there, put in by the previous owners. But that horse being so tame acting and all, he could belong to someone out here."

"Belong to someone? How could he belong to some-one?" asked Roger. He looked like someone had just handed him a treasure map to someone else's fortune.

"Well he could have got loose and just took up with that little herd. Or maybe somebody just turned him out."

"Turned him out?" said Roger. "Do people just turn horses out by themselves when they're not used to being on their own?"

"You'd think that the owners would at least try to find him a home, if he's a decent horse, or try to make some money by selling him, but you see all kinds of things in this world Roger. People don't always do the right thing, that's for sure."

Buck sat down by me after he had got up to accept a

second piece of pie from Mom. Sniffy came up to him and rubbed on his legs. I noticed that his legs were sort of long and not too fat or not too skinny above his dark boots.

"What's his name?" he asked.

"Sniffy," I said. "He's sort of crabby sometimes but he's funny when he is. And he still likes us a lot."

I wondered if I sounded dumb saying that. No, there was nothing wrong with what I said. I think at that point, I could have thought up the Declaration of Independence, and probably would have worried that I sounded like a moron.

"My sister had a rabbit with that name," he said smiling, as he took a bite of pie.

I started to say something to him, but Roger looked at Buck and said, "Do you think that horse will be okay? Do you think he will be okay Mr. Newman? I mean if he's just lost or abandoned?"

"Oh he'll probably do okay, said Mr. Newman. The wild ones seem to fare well. There's enough grazing and enough water between here and the Pine Nut Mountains. The only thing is, for a horse to live a long and healthy life, they should have their necessary shots and worm medicine. Their feet need to be taken care of, too. Now take Old Smoke, for instance. Ever since my wife Edna passed away I've had to make sure that her horse -she called him Smokey Blue- has his feet trimmed just right for him to stand proper, since he's had some trouble with the bones in one foot. He needs to have fly spray on him since he's developed a real irritation to their bites. When they get old like Smoke, they need to be babied some too, that's for sure. He's gonna be twenty-seven in May. Never thought he'd outlive Edna like this...never thought that would happen..." Mr. Newman shook his head.

Everyone was quiet for a minute until Mr. Newman spoke again.

"Yep. Taking care of a horse the right way is a real science, and being a good farrier is an art. Why I hope my foot doctor would know as much about my feet as my shoer knows about Old Smoke's," he said with a twinkle in his eye.

We enjoyed talking with Mr. Newman for the rest of the evening. We loved to listen to his stories about the Valley, both past and present. It was doubly interesting to talk to him, because we knew that he told the truth. He had a real love of God, and sense of humor to match. As time went on, I noticed how he brought a positive cloud of stability to the neighborhood. He had leaned on God while growing older, instead of just behaving how he felt and deciding to do something just from the way that the wind blew.

We talked on for a while longer until Roger yawned, and then got Mom and I yawning. Even Ford looked sleepy. He had been laying at Mr. Newman's feet all evening waiting for him to scratch him now and then on his back with the toe of his brown and tan leather boots.

"Well, thanks so much Katy, for the great pie. It was the best I've had in a long time."

"You're so welcome, Sam. Come over again before too long, won't you?"

"Thank you Mrs. Bloomingson." Buck said as he smiled at Mom, and Dad shook his hand again.

"You come back again too, Buck, "she said.

"I sure will. Goodnight everybody. Thanks again."

Buck hadn't said a lot that evening. I think it was because he didn't know us that well, but also I think he didn't want to talk over his grandfather. He seemed to really listen to him with as much interest as we did. I didn't say much either, but the whole time he was there, I felt some kind of invisible mist in the air. It was almost like the evening had a flavor, like when you get your favorite ice cream out of all thirty-one flavors, and it leaves you happy and satisfied even when you're done eating it.

"Bye Mr. Newman. Bye Buck! See you tomorrow," Roger called after them.

"Okay Roger. Time for bed," said Dad.

"Phooey!" Said Roger. "It seems like it's ALWAYS time for bed."

"It only seems that way because you're nine years old," laughed Dad.

Roger tried to look very grim and disgusted but he couldn't keep from laughing when Dad picked him up and swung him through the air and hung him over his shoulder as he walked down the hall. "Tickle me!

Tickle me!" he pleaded.

"Not tonight! It's too late. But I'll get you later during the daytime. You better be ready!"

Roger screeched with delight. "I will! I will!"

The warmth of the evening from Buck and Mr. Newman's visit and the talk of the beautiful little horse and the herd of mustangs, left Roger and I with a warm glow. We went to bed that night in anticipation of tomorrow being a great day.

6

Little Paint

The next morning Roger and I didn't have to be at school until eleven o'clock because of a special testing day in our classes. The whole school district was doing it. Mom was driving us in on her way to town, instead of us taking the buses. She had packed an "extra-super-duper lunch" for Roger, as he called it, since he had been doing his chores around the house so well and had been co-operating with me about stacking the wood-pile instead of his usual griping that "the other kids up the street that were his age didn't have to do woodpile stuff." If it was something fun or dangerous for him to do, he griped that "all the other kids but him got to do it." He had sure been annoying off and on lately.

Mom gave him two chocolate chip cookies in his lunch, and a new softball for a special surprise for him to bring with his new mitt to use at recess. She gave me some cookies too, and surprised me with some special sketching pens and sumi brushes that I had wanted. They weren't required for my art classes, but I would be able to have my own brushes with me to use whenever I needed them. I wouldn't have to wait to check out the well-worn ones in the art supply closet at school. A good sumi brush made all the difference to me, and drawing and painting were the two things that I looked forward to doing the most, in school or out. Good old Mom. Even though I was older, she didn't seem to favor Roger a lot over me just because he was younger, even though it would have been okay with me, unless he was being a real stinker.

Mom had just finished packing our lunches when she saw out of the back window, the little brown and white horse that Roger had seen the day before.

"Kids! Come quick!" she yelled toward the bedrooms.

Roger had just finished putting his socks on and came running out to the kitchen.

"Look out the window! Quick!"

"Ohhhh! There he is!" said Roger. " I'm going out to see him."

"Walk slowly," said Mom. "And be quiet."

Roger went out the back door in his socks. I watched him through the screen door while I went to get some carrots. He saw Mr. Newman at the side of his yard bending over a piece of wire fence and talking to Old Smoke.

"Mr. Newman! Mr. Newman!" he yelled in a loud whisper. "He's here! He's back again!"

Mr. Newman looked up and saw the little horse

standing in the middle of the hardy sagebrush, munching on the clumps of grass that grew in between them. "Well let's go over and meet the little feller."

"Where's Buck?" asked Roger. "I wanted him to see him too!"

He's up the road loading some wood for me at the Blayne's place. He'll be back though!"

They both walked slowly, without saying anything until they reached the back corral fence. The little horse went on eating and didn't look up right away. He was closer to this end of the yard this time so Roger and Mr. Newman could get a good look at him.

"Wow! He's really pretty!" said Roger to Mr. Newman.

"He sure is, Roger. He's a nicely built little horse. Looks real healthy."

"What kind of a horse do you think he is, Mr. Newman?"

"Well first of all, he's a gelding, not a stallion, so he was owned by someone once. His color is called overo Paint. He has a good-looking head. Looks like he could have some Quarter Horse and maybe some Arab in him. It's hard to tell with Paints. Especially when they're small like this. He's a good size for a pony though. Let's see. I estimate that he stands about thirteen hands high."

Mom and I came out of the house with two large carrots and walked slowly behind Mr. Newman. "Do you think he might come over to get these?" asked Mom.

"It's worth a try," he said.

I hung my carrot over the fence and Mom gave the other one to Roger.

Mr. Newman gave the horse a whistle and got his immediate attention. He had been eyeing everyone at the fence while still eating, ever since Mom and I had come out. Now he stopped eating and looked at the carrot without a doubt or worry. The friendly little horse walked over to the fence, took the carrot in his mouth and chewed it up until it was gone, just as if he had been born and raised on our property.

"He ate it!" Roger whispered to me. "Here's mine too, old boy," he said to the horse.

The small Paint liked the second carrot just as well as the first and ate it with enthusiasm.

"Boy does he have big teeth!" I said.

"He sure does!" said Roger in admiration. "Is it okay if we try to pet him?"

"Sure," said Mr. Newman.

Roger put his hand over the fence as far as he could reach and gave the horse a pat on his neck. He looked at Roger, and then he sniffed one of those long horse greetings. "Sniff- sniff- sniff- sniff- sniff- SNIFF!" Mr. Newman had shown Roger and I how horses greet each other that way. The first day that we had met Old Smoke, he had sniffed the same way towards Roger, then put his huge head on Roger's shoulder and rubbed his forehead and eyes on it until I thought Roger would fall over from the friendly, heavy, pushing weight.

Roger blew back at the little horse, as he stood there blinking huge coffee brown eyes.

"I think he likes you Roger," I said.

"I think so too," said Mom.

Mr. Newman just smiled. Then he looked closer at the horse's head and gave a surprised look.

"What's wrong, Mr. Newman?" said Roger.

"This horse has worn a halter recently," he said. "Look at those marks on him." He pointed at two little rust spots above the horse's left cheek on his white hair. "That looks like rust spots from an old halter buckle. This horse has probably been trained. I can't tell exactly how old he is, but for sure he's full-grown and doesn't look over ten years old. His feet have had shoes on at one time," he continued as he bent down to look at the hooves. "See the little holes on the edge of his hoof. They've grown out some, but they're old nail holes for sure. His feet have been trimmed in the not too distant past. He probably hasn't been running loose for too long."

"Mom." Roger looked at Mom. She knew what he wanted to ask her. "We'll see," she said. "Let's talk to Dad about it." Then she said to Mr. Newman, "How does a person adopt a lost or wild horse, Sam? I've heard of some sort of program where you can do that."

"Well you have to contact the BLM."

"What's that?" I said.

"The Bureau of Land Management - government landholdings. That's what the Pine Nut Mountains are, and the wild horses that live there are protected under government law." I can get a hold of the brand inspector and ask him about it"

"Could we Mom? Oh could we?" asked Roger.

"We'll see, we'll see. Remember, I said we'll talk to Dad." She gave him a big smile, and I could see a little shiny spot in each of her eyes.

"Okay!" Said Roger. He walked quietly away from the corral fence so as not to disturb the little Paint horse. Then he jumped up into the air with hands and feet flying, "Great! This is so great!"

That night our family discussed the possibilities of adopting the friendly little horse and it seemed that Dad thought, "It just might be a good idea."

"Mr. Newman does know a lot about horses Dad. He said he could help me get old Paint's training back into shape. He promised me that he would." Roger looked like he was immensely happy, but that he might cry, all at the same time.

"Okay Roger, we'll talk to the Bureau of Land Management and see what they say. We have to find out about their rules and regulations. I wouldn't normally keep a horse that we don't know anything about, but since Mr. Newman would be helping us, it might work out all right."

It just seemed as though God had answered Roger's prayer just like that. Just like a snap! Roger was so happy that night that he could hardly go to sleep.

"Mom," I called from my room. "Roger keeps making

swooshing and grunting noises."

"Settle down and lay still Roger, so you can go to sleep."

"Okay Mom," he called.

But she didn't really say much. I could picture those little shiny spots in her eyes again, and I thought that it was probably kind of hard for her to settle down and go to sleep that night, too.

7

Failed Expectations

The next morning was, in striking contrast to the events of the day before, a dull gray.

Looks like we might be in for a thunderstorm," said Dad as he looked out the front living room window. "See those dark clouds over the hills?"

"Ooooh," said Mom. "It does look a little threatening doesn't it?"

Time to go," said Dad. He gave Mom a kiss and a big hug then went out the front door to his truck. "See you tonight."

"Bye," she called.

We were just waking up. All through the morning as Roger got ready for school he talked about the wonderful little Paint horse that he had discovered in his very own back pasture and how he thought that God had meant for him to have him - like he was just brought here.

It was hard to get through school that day. Roger was in a lather to spot that horse in our yard again. By the time that we were dropped off of the buses near our house, Roger could hardly wait to make it to the backyard to see if the horse was still there. He was. The little Paint had decided to stay. I was glad to be home too. I was hoping that Buck was still staying there at Mr. Newman's.

I heard voices, and walked around the side of the house. Mr. Newman was out there with Buck talking to the mailman.

Mr. Newman had a serious look on his face. "So you say they're coming back to the valley to get him on Saturday?"

"That's what they told their neighbors," said the mailman. "Their neighbors had said that they'd keep an eye out for the Stone's horse. He disappeared from the Stone's place right after they left for vacation about a month ago. Someone let him out of their back pasture, but the neighbors who were feeding him, didn't see anything.

"Who's coming back?" said Roger. "Who's coming back to get who?"

"Roger," said Mr. Newman, "the little horse got loose from his owners about a month ago when they were on vacation. Someone opened the gate to his corral. The neighbors who were feeding him didn't know where to look. He must have gone off with the small herd that's been coming through here in the afternoons and evenings, and then he ended up here in your backyard these last few days. I guess he doesn't like to be on the move so much."

"I guess not," said Roger as he walked slowly away from the three men.

"Are you okay Roger?" Buck called after him.

Roger went towards the house before the tears that were building up in his eyes could roll down his face in two huge dust-lined streams.

"Roger, you'll be okay," I said. I didn't know what else to say. He looked terrible and I felt so bad for him. I put my arm around him. "Mom," I called toward the house. "Mom! Let's go talk to her for a minute."

When we went into the kitchen, Mom bent down and put her arms around him too and said," What's wrong cowboy?"

Roger put his face on her shoulder and cried for quite a while. In between sobs, he told Mom the story about the lost horse having owners, and that Saturday they were coming back for him.

"And I thought God wanted me to have that horse! I thought he was for me!" Roger was all of a sudden very angry. He ran into his room and shut the door very hard but it bounced back open.

"It's okay Lissy," said Mom. "I'll talk to him in a few minutes."

Roger was in his room pouting and sulking. Then he cried a little bit. Then he picked up a comic book off of his bed and threw it onto the floor. Then he stamped his foot and started crying again. I knew that he shouldn't be doing that. Mom had talked to him about that before.

He even sounded kind of silly in there making a ruckus and moaning and growling. I poked my head into the doorway. He looked at me out of red bleary eyes and said, "Lissy!" Then he sat on his floor by the bed.

I came in and he told me that all sorts of crazy angry things were going through his mind. He could take the horse and run off and hide someplace, but he didn't know where to go. The people would just come back again to our house probably, so it wouldn't do any good anyway. But he said that these weren't the real reasons that kept him from doing that. We would all worry about him, and also, it was just plain wrong. He had no desire to be the youngest horse rustler in all of Carson Valley.

After he had calmed down he felt very sorry because he realized that he had been angry with God. He said to me between little sobbing breaths, "I've been...terrible. I was mad at God I think. Do you think He's m..mad at me?"

"Are you sorry?" I asked.

"Yes," he said.

"And you don't want to do it again?"

"Nope."

"You're forgiven."

"Okay," he said.

"You know how Jesus saved us from our sins?" I said to Roger.

"Right," he said.

"Well, he can save us from being dumb, too. And

He's told us that he uses all these things for our own good and sometimes has something better for us, so we don't have to feel so horrible and be so dumb. Me and you, I mean."

Me, with diplomacy with my brother! Good things were happening. I didn't know, though, that I would be struggling with this very thing myself, before too long - being dumb, and feeling sorry for myself.

As Roger got ready for bed that night, splashing his toothpaste as usual all over his side of the mirror, and dripping mouthwash on the counter between our sinks, he told me that he felt better. But he was still asking, "Why did the horse come to our backyard? Why was he running around by himself like that? Why did he find US? Why, why, why?"

I wondered when he wouldn't be so sloppy brushing his teeth and when he would remember to wipe the counter off after himself without being told, so it wouldn't be such a mess for me to use, but then, I guess I'm just too practical. At least where Roger's concerned.

8

Double Calamity

Roger still had three more gut wrenching days to go, before the horse that had grabbed his cowboy heart by the bootstraps was to be taken out of our yard, and away from him forever.

I didn't know that today was not going to be the greatest day in my life either. It was bright and sunny, almost as if the approaching warmth of summer was being grabbed by a huge hand and pulled on to get here sooner than it was expected to.

We had dressed early and eaten breakfast almost before the sun was up. Roger and I had gone out to look at the little horse again, and brought him the two biggest carrots that we could find in the refrigerator vegetable keeper.

"Well I guess it's going to be so long, old boy," said Roger sadly.

We heard feet walking up behind us from Mr. Newman's place, and I knew it must be Buck, because whoever it was, was walking fast and spry, and Mr.

Newman had a slight limp from arthritis and moved slower. Today I had that same good flavored mist feeling that I had the other night, just before I turned around to face Buck. This time I was going to be brave, and coolly say with an almost lazy nonchalance and a big attractive smile, 'Oh, hi, Buck.'

Then before I could even get myself turned around, I heard, "Oh Buck, he is a cute little pony, just like you said."

The voice came from a girl, not a lot taller than I was, but older than Buck and I both, being a Senior at our school. She looked out of her blue eyes at everyone else, as if she was looking in a mirror. As if everything she said was measured so carefully to look smart and cute and good. Her short yellow blond hair was real, but I couldn't accept her sugary sweet friendliness to us as ANYTHING but perfumed horse manure, like the kind of smell that comes from strongly scented bath-room spray.

"And these are the two cute little neighbors that you told me about!"

Oh please… I could hardly stand this. I didn't like her already and she had been in my yard less than ten seconds. She was just too phony with a phony good-lookingness. Or was it just that she was standing next to Buck as if she was his best friend and fiancée or something, acting like I was just a little kid!

"I'm Lisbeth Bloomingson," I said, almost with a fierce dignity. This is my younger brother Roger."

I wanted to make a clear distinction between 'little' Roger and 'mature' me.

'Hi. . !" the girl said. She smiled at us, then smiled up at Buck then looked back at us. "I'm Pearl Blayne," she said, in a way that a beauty pageant host would have announced.

She spoke again. "Oh I have to go now, Buck. I'm late for practice."

Leaving already, I thought. What did you come over for? Just to stand here and look old next to me?

Pearl, or "Peachy" as some of her friends would call her, as if Pearl wasn't a peachy enough name to roll around and revel in when you looked like a squatty Barbie doll with pink cheeks, was on her way to eighteen years old, but acted like she had seen the sunrises and sunsets of a well-seasoned twenty-seven. Buck, at least six months her junior, was old enough to hold her interest, I thought, probably because of his adult demeanor, and nice looks. It seemed like she would have been attracted to somebody older and more cool and 'macho acting' than Buck. She was too dumb to appreciate the finer points of a guy with character, and a 'goodness' with how he dealt with even immature and pesty little people like Roger. Or was she?

"I have 'cheer' practice," she said very businesslike to Buck. I found out later, that she wasn't a cheerleader at school, but some sort of song leader for pep rallies at the high school, which weren't my cup of tea either.

"Okay," said Buck. "I'm driving in to school early

today myself. I can give you a ride."

"Thank you… I appreciate it so… much," she said in her dreamy fashion. She thanked Buck as if he had just saved her from falling off of a cliff. I was glad they were leaving.

Buck walked over and patted the little horse on the cheek. "You're a good old guy, aren't you," he said, scratching him around the ears and forehead. The horse liked the attention. He seemed to like Buck too.

"Well just thought I'd check to see how you were all doing," said Buck with a smile. "See you later."

"Bye Buck!" said Roger.

As the two of them walked away, "Peachy" grabbed onto Bucks arm, as if she needed some help walking across the ever so smooth stretch of grass and dirt between our houses. What a way to start the morning, I lamented to myself.

When we were alone again, Roger said, while still petting the little horse, "Boy, she's kind of weird, isn't she?"

I was so annoyed, I couldn't even talk about it.

"What's the matter?" he said.

"Ohhh… nothing!" I was in a foul mood, and went into the house.

Buck drove Pearl off to her 'cheer practice' in his Chevy truck. He had got his learner's permit at fifteen, and his license at sixteen, like all the other kids at school, even though he had been driving for more than three years before that. He lived on a modest sized ranch called "Little Mountain," or "L/M" Ranch, on the southeast side of our valley where his Dad raised alfalfa and cattle. Buck had driven trucks and tractors and farm equipment since he was twelve, through the fields and on the unpaved back roads of the Carson Valley. 'She' must have latched onto him I thought, when he went to her house to load the wood that Mr. Newman had bought from her Dad, Mr. Blayne.

I sat in my room in misery. I could never compete against a squatty Barbie doll who looked so much older than me in a 'vampy' sort of way. And it had looked like our move out to Nevada wasn't going to be so bad after all. In fact, it had looked pretty hopeful that Roger and I would be glad that we moved here. But now, he was losing 'his' horse and I was losing my ... well, now, he wasn't 'my' guy, but in the craziest imagination of my hopeful heart, I had thought that maybe some day, Whether 'Buck' Alvie MacCleod, might think a lot of me, or maybe even half, of what I thought of him.

I fell over on my bed, stuck my head under my pillow and cried.

9

Battle Ground

Mr. Newman had asked the mailman to leave a note at the house of the people who owned the little brown and white horse so they would know where to come today to pick him up. All we could do at our house was wait. Even Mom and Dad were a little on edge about things. Then at about one o'clock that afternoon, we heard a truck pull into our driveway. Dad and Mr. Newman had been talking in the front yard.

A man got out of the white pickup. He was tall with black hair and wore cowboy boots and a black western hat.

"Howdy there! he said in a friendly voice.

He introduced himself as Ted James, the brand inspector for Douglas County. Mr. Newman knew him and liked him. They talked for a while with Dad and then got down to business. The owners of the little Paint hadn't showed up. They were four hours late. The brand inspector suggested that he and Dad drive over to the house of these phantom people who had so greatly affected our lives for the last week, that we hadn't even seen yet, and knew nothing at all about.

Mr. Newman knew that the wait was pretty hard on Roger, so he invited him to go shooting out in the Pine Nuts. Roger would just go to watch, with him and Buck, and 'the Blayne girl.' "I already talked to your Dad about it and it's all right if you go," he said.

I stood there with a sick feeling in my stomach, and was surprised when Mr. Newman said, "You're welcome to come along too, Lissy."

Go along too? How would that be? Could I stand it? Could I stand not to go?

"Okay," I said. Did I say that? How did I have such a calm smile on my face?

"Alright then, grab your jackets – you might need them later - and let's get going!"

"Okay, Mr. Newman," said Roger. He looked glad to go, but not *real* glad. Nothing could get him that excited today.

I changed my clothes very quickly. I threw on my cornflower blue jeans with my light yellow blouse with the blue tulips embroidered on the front. I liked that outfit because it had my favorite colors. I felt good in it. It helped to have something on that I felt good in.

Roger and I jumped into the back of the pickup after getting our jackets and settled ourselves down into the two front corners behind the cab. Mr. Newman said we could ride in back because we would be driving slowly through the sand pits and then out the dirt roads that led into the wilderness where people could shoot their guns. We needed to find a good spot up against a hill, where we could see where the bullets' final resting places would be, and that no people or animals were in the way.

Buck and Pearl came out of Mr. Newman's house and got into the front of the cab with Mr. Newman. Buck carried a .22 rifle with him and gave a little wave to us as he got in. Pearl gave a little side-glance and tossed her head, as if to say, I saw you, but I'm a little busy right now.

She made me feel so young - like I was ten years old.

In less than ten minutes, we were out in the rolling Pine Nut Mountains. Jackrabbits scattered here and there at the sound of our truck, or probably from the vibration, even before we got close to them. Dead, dried up skeletons of little things, mostly rabbits and squirrels, occasionally broke the sameness of each scene around the bend. Pinion Pines, Russian Thistle, Rabbit Brush, and Sagebrush by the thousands, stood their ground as they had done for who knows how many years before, for as far as we could see.

We drove for a little while longer when Mr. Newman hollered back at us, "We're almost there, kids!"

Roger and I looked at each other. Neither one of us felt very inspired about being 'almost there." I gave Roger a little smile. He just looked at me with his sad brown eyes. He soaked up my smile like he appreciated the sympathy and said thank you without any words.

A huge cracking sound broke the air around us. It sounded like a piece of building breaking off suddenly. But not exactly. Or like a piece of thunder kept bottled up in a lead vault and then let out all at once. Then we heard it again.

Mr. Newman stopped the truck. He sat there very still for a minute. He looked all the way around us, then back in the direction we were pointed in. He started driving slowly. I figured he must have been deciding what to do. Maybe turn around, maybe go on to see what was causing the noise. He stopped the truck again and got out.

"Lissy and Roger, you two get down in the truck bed and stay there. Buck and Pearl will stay in the cab." He looked very serious. We knew we better do what he said.

He walked over behind a small clump of pine trees and looked down the slope into the next small valley that we would be going into when we followed the curve of the dirt road. He watched for a few minutes, then came back to the truck.

Buck got out of the truck.

Mr. Newman said to him, "A truck just pulled away. I'm hoping they were just target practicing down there. But that's a pretty big gun they're using. We'll just take it slow. I'll turn around if it doesn't look like we should be there." He kept talking to Buck while they got back into the truck. "There's something that looks like a corral down there. That bothers me... "

We went up the dirt road, around the curve, and into the small valley. There was something like a corral up ahead. It was broken down, with one side missing.

Roger looked more interested now than he had been in the last two weeks. He got up on his knees, pointed his hand towards the bottom of the upper bank that we had just come from, and said, "Look!"

Standing there by themselves was a large but very skinny foal, brown, and dirt covered, and a little steer about six months old. We drove closer, and could see that the steer had sores on his back, and the foals eyes were runny, like I had seen on Ford once when he had a cold. I had to make myself very stiff to overcome the sadness that was gripping me. Roger said quietly to me, "Look at them, Lissy."

All we could do was stare at them. I thought I saw the foal shaking a little. Or was it just me? We all got out and looked at the two animals. They were in such bad shape that they didn't even try to walk away.

"What happened to them Mr. Newman?" said Roger.

"I'm not sure, Roger, but there's something wrong. There's not a good smell in the air." We noticed it too, but didn't know what it was.

"What do we do, Grandpa?" said Buck.

"Let's go to the Seller's place. We can take that south road there. The little steer might belong to them. The horse is probably wild, and maybe an orphan." They can come and get the steer and maybe the little horse too. He could go to animal control for now, then the BLM adoption center.

"Good," said Buck. "I'm glad we can do something for them." Buck spoke for all of us, and it gave us some relief for the way we felt about the two little 'critters,' as Mr. Newman called them. All of us, except for Pearl.

"But I thought we were going shooting!" It's so far to drive to that place... the Sellers. Why can't we leave the wild animals to fend for themselves? They should be okay." She tucked her little chin into her neck with a little 'pout' look and grabbed on to Buck's arm.

Buck didn't say anything, but just had sort of a blank stare on his face.

Mr. Newman didn't even answer her. He just said, "Let's get in the truck, kids."

We drove past the little horse and steer slowly and Mr. Newman circled the truck around the flat space of the corral area. Then we all saw, on the other side of some rocks and sagebrush, the bodies of two adult mares. They had been there awhile, according to Mr. Newman because they were somewhat dried up and the smell wasn't as strong as it could have been. At the same time, we also heard the sound of another engine moving quickly towards us from around the turn that went the other direction out of the valley.

A bluish gray truck was pulling a stock trailer. Two guys were in it. "Well, hello... to you!" said the older one. He acted funny. Mr. Newman got out of the truck.

Buck did too, but he stayed close to it, with his arm inside the door near Pearl.

"Well what are you two young fellers doing around here," said Mr. Newman in a friendly way. But he didn't sound like he usually did.

"Just relaxing with a little target practice, that's all." The younger boy, who was high school age, didn't say anything. He looked quietly nervous.

"Sounds like you've got a pretty big gun there, for target practice.

"30-ought-6," said the older guy with haughtiness.

The two of them got out of the truck. They were dressed almost like cowboys, but sloppy. They hadn't shaved for a few days, and the older one had a can of beer in his hand. Everyone in our truck began to get a little nervous. Even Roger, who's usually Mr. "Hey what's going on?" knew that something was wrong.

Mr. Newman looked over at the dead mares. He looked at the stock trailer. It had live animals in it. Little steers. Too many, he told us later, to be in one trailer.

"Hey, don't get us wrong, gramps," the older guy said, waving his beer can towards the bodies, "we didn't do that - at least not both of them. One of them was sick. It would have died anyway. The other one had a nasty temper."

I had the feeling that if he hadn't been drinking a lot, he wouldn't have told us any of this.

The younger, nervous guy finally said, "Cut it out

Earl, let's just go."

"No, we came out to fix the corral and unload our stock."

He seemed determined, and walked to the back of the trailer. He said to the younger guy, "Don't worry about an old guy and kids, Dirk."

Dirk said nervously to Mr. Newman. "We work for the Seller's."

"Okay, Dirk," said Earl, "back the trailer into the corral. I'll get the fence up. Go ahead and look around," he said to Mr. Newman. "You won't bother us." He acted like he was the owner of the place, and all of this sagebrush property was part of his homestead.

As Earl walked past Mr. Newman's truck, he looked past Buck, into the pickup. "Well what do you know," he said. "Hi there, Pearl."

Pearl sat there a minute looking straight ahead, then said a quick, quiet, "Hi."

'How've you been," said Earl.

"Okay, I guess," she said. She looked embarrassed and sort of miserable.

How creepy to know someone like that, I thought. I wondered what went on with them. He looked like too much for even Pearl to handle. I almost felt sorry for her.

"Don't unload those cattle!" It was a direct command.

Mr. Newman stood there stiffly, after saying that to Earl, and then waving his hand toward his truck, he said, "Buck!"

Buck immediately pulled out the twenty-two and fired a shot into the air.

"Get out!" Mr. Newman said to Dirk in the truck. "Now!"

"You…!" he said to Earl, "…over there with your friend! Now both of you into the bed of your truck!"

"What, do you think you're doing, old man!" said Earl.

"This old man," said Mr. Newman, "knows that those aren't your cattle, and most likely, not your truck either! Get in the back of the truck, like I said. I'd do it if I were you. Buck's a pretty good shot."

Earl didn't look so much dangerous right now, as he did snaky. He looked tired and drunk, and Dirk just looked scared spitless. So they got into the pickup bed.

"We're going to the Sellers' place," said Mr. Newman.

Buck handed the twenty-two to Mr. Newman. He got into the cab of the other guys' truck. He would be driving them to the Sellers' place, while Mr. Newman held the gun on them from his truck.

Mr. Newman told Roger and I to get into the cab with him and Pearl. He kept the .22 pointed towards the two sullen scoundrels while he told Pearl, "I need you to drive."

Pearl looked like she had just swallowed a whole Brussels sprout, and it had stuck halfway down between her teeth and her stomach. "But I'm not very good on a stick shift, Mr. Newman! I haven't learned that much about driving trucks and things like this yet!"

"Pearl," he said. "Have you heard of instant oatmeal?"

"Of course," she said. "I don't eat it though."

"Well, you're going to eat a whole bowl of it today. Get behind the wheel and learn to start driving very quickly."

"I'll drive you Mr. Newman!" said Roger. "I'll do it for you!"

"Believe me, Roger," he said, "if you could reach the pedals better, you'd be the one driving!"

Pearl had a tight grip on the wheel with one hand, and her other hand seemed glued to the gearshift like her life was at stake. The truck lurched forward then died. She started it again. It lurched two more times, then seemed to even out a little as we moved in gentle jerks, then one long rumble, along the dirt road.

"Keep 'er steady, there Pearl, you're doing good," said Mr. Newman.

Roger looked happier than I'd seen him look all week when Mr. Newman had told him that he wished Roger could be driving.

Mr. Newman looked weary. It had been stressful on all of us, dealing with those two scary and unpleasant people, and seeing the dead horses and pitiful little orphans. But I think it was the hardest on Mr. Newman, because he felt responsible for all of us, and for needing to do the right thing. We found out later that one reason he stayed to bring those two back at gunpoint was, he didn't know if they might just take a hankering to do some target practice on us as we were driving away. They knew Mr. Newman was on to them.

The Sellers' ranch was a large spread, with lots of corrals and outbuildings, and a good-sized ranch house.

Pearl looked like she had just swallowed a whole Brussels sprout.....

Two of the ranch hands were standing near a tractor, looking at the engine when they saw our strange caravan drive up. Their faces changed from pleasant puttering talk to serious stares when they saw Mr. Newman and his rifle hanging out the window.

"Go get Floyd for me will you fellers!" Mr. Newman called to the men.

They went quickly to the large brown wood barn and brought back Mr. Sellers.

Buck had jumped out of the truck when we got there. He had the 30-ought-6 in his hands, so it wouldn't fall into the wrong ones again.

Mr. Sellers came running out of the barn at a high speed for a man over sixty. "What's happenin' Sam?" he said to Mr. Newman. "Hey that's my rig there," he said to Buck. "It's been gone two days, but I thought Lefty had it down by the south pasture."

Mr. Newman explained what we had seen today to Mr. Sellers. Mr. Sellers looked over at Earl and Dirk and said, "I fired those two last week! So that's where my rig was!"

The men on the ranch that found out what was going on all gathered around Earl and Dirk and helped to keep the two unhappy culprits from making any more trouble until the sheriff came.

After all of them had compared notes with Mr. Newman, they realized that Earl and Dirk had been stealing rigs for a day or two, and taking cattle from Washoe County. Then they would bring them to Carson

Valley back in the Pine Nuts where they met a truck from California, which had just recently been caught, that would transport the beef to various farther away places. Mr. Newman had talked to the brand inspector last week and knew that this stuff had been going on for months, even though they hadn't found everybody who was involved in it yet. He also knew that the white and black cattle that were in the stock trailer weren't Mr. Sellers', but he thought he recognized the truck. The two boys were not good to the animals, and had degraded even farther into horse thievery for "resale," sometimes to slaughter houses, and sometimes shooting to kill, just for the fun of it. The dead mares were wild, and harder for thieves to deal with. The little orphans were probably offspring of some of the older dead or stolen animals. The little brown and white horse in our back pasture had disappeared from his yard at the same time that a few other horses in our area had been reported missing. Then thankfully, he escaped later from one of their makeshift corrals out in the desert.

There wasn't a whole lot more for any of us to do, so we took off for home with Mr. Newman. We were all squeezed into the large truck cab, with Roger stuffed behind the seat in a small storage space. I sat between Mr. Newman and Pearl, with Buck by the door.

Everyone was quiet as we drove down the dusty roads. Then Roger, breaking the quiet, said, "Pearl, do you really know that guy?"

I thought my teeth would fall out when I heard

him say that. Roger, what an idiotic thing to say right then!

Pearl just quietly said, "Well, we went out a few times. But I didn't really like him. 'Least not after the last time I was with him."

She turned her head to look out the window past Buck, but I could see that her eyes were starting to get a little teary, and she was really upset.

Nobody said anything for a minute, until I surprised myself and said, "I knew a guy back in Walnut Creek, in school. Then I found out he wasn't too great." I hoped I didn't sound too awkward or silly, or like I had liked horrible people or something, but I just felt sorry for Pearl. It made me feel a little older too.

She didn't say anything back. She just sat there and sniffed. Pearl wasn't the kind to suck up kindness and bestow huge thanks upon people. She just took it. But for an instant, Buck glanced over at me and gave me a little smile.

10

Nevada Sage

When we got back to the house, Dad and Mom were talking to the brand inspector in the front yard. Mr. Newman told them what had happened, with Roger putting his two cents in now and then. Then Roger remembered the little horse that had been on his mind all day, until his thoughts had been taken over by the cattle rustlers. "Did the people come to get old Paint yet?" he said with a weary sadness.

Dad said, "Well, not exactly."

Ted James shifted his black Stetson hat, then looked at Roger and said, "The people who had the horse taken from them by those two varmints, are moving to a place in California where they can't keep horses. They brought him over to a house up the street. The Evans' place. A girl named Deedee lives there. She's about your age, isn't she? Your dad said that you know her."

"Oh, Deedee," said Roger. "They're giving him to Deedee?"

"I guess so," said Mr. James. "I was going to tell them

about you, but it looks like they had it all worked out already."

"Oh," said Roger.

"Dad looked at Roger with a worried frown. "Well, thanks for all your help, Ted," he said quickly. Roger wasn't in any shape for cordial thank-yous.

"You want to go in with Buck and me and get something to eat?" I said to Roger. "I'm starving."

"I guess," he said, and he started walking towards the house.

"Hey Roger!" We saw a boy that was yelling to Roger on his bicycle up the road. "Roger! My Dad wants you to come up to our house for a minute. Deedee wants to show you something!" It was Deedee's older brother Jeff. "He wants your Dad to come too."

Roger just looked at Dad like he wanted to be rescued from the whole thing, but he was friends with Deedee and she had always been nice to him, so he said a quiet little, "Okay," from a droopy little mouth that reminded me of a depressed toad.

"I'll drive you up there in the truck," said Buck. He shook the spare set of keys that he had from his grandfather's truck a little nervously in his hands. I could tell that he cared about Roger too. More than a lot of guys his age would. "You want to go too Lissy?"

"Sure," I said. Starving, or not, Roger needed our moral support now, more than ever before.

We got into the truck, and Dad drove up in his car. Pearl had buzzed home quickly, having no more interest in any of us. I was glad she left, brushing off her clothes, and taking with her a dusty crabbiness that I didn't want to be around anyway.

When we got to Deedee's, we could see the horse in their backyard. Roger stiffened. Wow, what a tough thing for such a little guy, I thought. Why did God let it go this way, I wondered. I just didn't understand it. I don't think any of us did.

"Hi Roger!" Deedee said. She was a dainty little thing. She was dressed in an emerald green dress with matching green hair ribbons. Her shoulder length dark brown hair matched her eyes that were as round as buttons on the face of a Teddy Bear. This is the new owner of the Paint horse? How strange life can be.

Dad and Deedee's father, Mr. Evans, greeted each other when we got to the back yard, and shook hands and did all the parent talk that Dad's do when they meet.

My stomach was growling. I hoped nobody heard it. My being hungry seemed sort of heartless to me at a time like this.

Roger went up to the little Paint and patted him on the neck. The horse gave him a little nudge back with his nose on his arm. Roger looked at Buck and I and gave us a sad little smile.

"Well Paul," said Mr. Evans, "Deedee has something to ask Roger, and I wanted you to be here to see if it's okay."

He started talking quietly to Dad for a minute, but

before he was done, Deedee began telling Roger, "Some friends of ours are moving and they need to find a home for Sagebrush here, and they were going to give him to some friends in Placerville, but I told them that I have a friend who loves horses and he's wanted one for oh, just years and years!" she said, without hardly taking a breath, "and they said to me that if you didn't want him, for me to keep him, but I told them that I thought you would like him and, well… do you, want him, I mean…? She trailed off, studying Roger, because he just stood there with a, how can I say it without sounding mean, but a really stupid look on his face.

Deedee's Great Aunt Bertie had just come out of the house and was looking at Deedee and Roger with a big smile.

Suddenly, Roger looked like a light beam had just shot through him. "Me?" he said. "Me? You got him for me?"

Deedee stared at him with the corners of her mouth turned up into a puzzled grin. "Sure," she said.

"Why that's all she's talked about all day," said Aunt Bertie. "I've never seen a little girl so excited about any-thing before in my life! She's just the sweetest little thing. Why you ought to give her a nice big kiss for that!"

Aunt Bertie was old and roly-poly and a little comi-cal looking the way she talked, but I didn't think she would be that deranged to think that Roger would want to KISS Deedee!

"What?" said Roger. He was in shock. Euphoria and horror all at once was a difficult thing to grapple with. He was being offered a chocolate cupcake with a bug on it. Do you accept the cupcake and swipe the bug off, or eat around the bug and try to pretend it's not there to not be rude, or don't eat the cupcake at all…?

"Oh he doesn't have to do that!…" said Deedee, twirling around in a circle, looking a little embarrassed, but really thrilled with the thought of it all. I was beginning to catch on. Deedee really LIKED Roger. She LIKED my goofy little brother!

I looked at Buck. We could both hardly keep from laughing. Dad and Deedee's father had embarrassed grins. I wondered what other havoc Aunt Bertie must wreak on their family when we're not even there.

Deedee continued, "but do you want to come over and play with me tomorrow? We can dig for termites in our old fence posts. There's a whole bunch of them in there and they made a lot of tunnels and stuff."

"I sure would!" Roger almost yelled. Relief was billowing off of him in such an avalanche, it was almost insulting, except that he added quickly, "Boy, you're just about the nicest girl that I've ever known!"

She just smiled at him. It seemed to be enough for her that he felt that way.

Roger looked at Buck and I. "He's mine! He's really really mine now! Thanks Deedee!"

"Go ahead and take him home," said Deedee's father. "You can have the tack that came with him too." He handed the end of the lead rope that was attached to the horse's halter to Roger.

"Wow!" said Roger. "I can hardly believe it!"

While Dad stayed and talked to Mr. Evans, and got the saddle and other tack to put in the car, Roger started leading the horse out to the front yard. He stopped for a minute, then he turned to Deedee. "Did you call him Sagebrush?" he asked.

"That's his name," she said.

"Oh," he said. "I like it." He started walking again, then stopped and turned to her. "Well you know what? I'd like to shake your hand."

"Okay," she said.

Roger took her hand, shook it quickly, then hustled off down her driveway with his new horse as quickly as he could without looking like he was actually running away.

We were so happy for Roger, and Buck and I were just about unglued by the time we got into the truck.

"Those two are a real case of beans," laughed Buck.

"I know," I said, laughing too. "Can you believe her actually LIKING Roger!"

"I'd like to shake your hand!" Buck said, still laughing, then he took my hand and shook it. We stopped shaking for just a fraction of a minute and looked at each other. Buck held my hand for a second, then he let go of it carefully. He got quiet and started up the truck. We rode home making a little polite talk until he dropped me off at my house.

"I'll see you later," he said. "I've got to stop by the Blayne's for a minute tonight before I come back to help Grandpa with something."

"Okay," I said. "Bye, Buck. Thanks for coming with us to Deedee's." Then he was gone. Back over to Pearl's.

I went into the house and told Mom what had happened with Roger and the horse.

Mom looked really happy. Almost like a girl again. She had ridden horses while growing up, and loved them too, and knew just how Roger felt.

That evening Roger and I were standing by the corral fence saying goodnight to Roger's new horse. We were bundled up in our jackets because it was getting pretty chilly, and were giving carrots to the newest member of our family.

"Roger," I said," are you just as happy with this horse as you would be with a horse that you could go pick out yourself? I mean, it's funny how he just showed up before you had a chance to look around or anything."

"I'm happier," he said. "I think he picked me out. Or at least God helped him pick me out. He's the neatest horse that ever was, I think!" And he hugged his horse around the neck. "He was only a wild horse for a little while, but it was still so exciting to find him in our back pasture! I'm going to call him Nevada, because if we didn't move here we never would have been able to have him. And he's already been called Sagebrush. Yep. I'm going to call him Nevada Sage, 'cause that's where we first saw each other and started being friends."

"Good idea," said a voice from behind us.

"Hi Buck," I said, as I turned around without even having to think what to say. I felt more comfortable around him. After all, we had been through a lot together today.

"Hi Tulip," he said, smiling.

"Tulip?" I said.

"Yeah," he said. "Like the ones on the blouse that you wore today."

Tulips? He remembered what I wore today?

"Oh, that's right," I said.

"I had to stop by the Blayne's house tonight so Mr. Blayne could pay me for the work that I've been doing for him," he said, "then I thought I'd come over here and see how things were going."

Can a person be extremely embarrassed but extremely happy about tulips, all at the same time?

As Buck came up to pat Nevada Sage on his neck and talk to Roger about him, I just stood there soaking up the contentment of the day. I was glad for Roger and I. God had helped us through this part of our journey, and He would help us through the rest. He really does answer prayers, even though sometimes it happens in round about ways. He had things all worked out for us during these difficult beginnings, even when things looked the worst. But who can figure out the way that God does everything, I thought, except that He loves us and has mighty power to hold even the atoms together and He isn't stuck in one little spot like people are.

"Hey, I hear that you like to draw," said Buck. "I like to take photographs. Maybe we could take some pictures of the scenery around here, and you could do some drawings from them. I've heard that's what the great artists would do sometimes. Before they had cameras, they'd even copy pictures of other artists to learn how to paint better."

"That sounds like a great idea to me," I said.

Great? What was I saying! It was spectacular! But I wouldn't let him know how spectacular I thought that idea was. Not right then. I would wait for the day when Buck MacCleod would think a lot of me, or maybe even half of what I thought of him. And just maybe there was a good chance of that happening after all.

11

Born to Ride

Roger was just born to ride. It almost seems like, when God was forming his innermost parts, Roger had been making plans on how to rope and ride, and itching to get into the saddle and make that grass cruncher move. Mom said that Roger jumped around a lot before he was born. I could imagine him taking notes in there from some unknown angel about how to swing a lasso, and how much hay to feed, and how to change leads on a canter. When he was a young toddler and could barely talk, he would want me to be his horse. "Slithy be horth," he would say. Since I was almost seven years older than him, I could run around on my hands and knees and give him a "horth lide."

Ever since Deedee had given Nevada Sage to Roger, I had watched him riding almost every day, and was in awe that my sometimes hair-brained little brother could do so well. He also took good care of his horse. He had learned how much hay to feed, and to make sure that Nevada had plenty of fresh water in his trough, and

Roger was just born to ride

to not go overboard on horse goodies or energy-laced molasses horse supplements. Roger studied the horse shoer's every move while he trimmed Nevada's feet and fired up his forge for heating the horseshoes. I remember in particular one day when Roger picked up a nail from the side shelf of the farrier truck and said, "Square nails! What a good idea! I bet they stick in there better!" I didn't know if they did or not, but he looked like he had just discovered a vaccine.

Now that was Roger. Nine years old and almost a candidate for the Austrian School of Lipizzaners. But with me, it was a different story.

I liked horses, especially Nevada Sage. He was a friendly little horse, and fun to ride. In the execution of dressage, he was good-natured and prone to being obedient, especially with Mr. Newman's help. "Make that hayburner do what you say, with your hands light on the reins, and remember your legs. Remember the cues. Those legs talk, you know. Toes forward, heels down. Sit up straight, but relaxed. You're looking good! You're looking good!" he would call to us as he leaned on our corral fence, shifting his khaki colored cap around better to block the sun. Mr. Newman was a great help to us, and we learned a lot, but I didn't have the same free and easy spirit as Roger did when it came to horses. Even though I had a good time, I wasn't real confident like Roger. Me, sixteen-year-old Lisbeth Bloomingson. Not the cowgirl I had hoped to be, under the clear Nevada sky, in the sight of the eagles and hawks and our vast ring of surrounding mountains. Out in a place like this you just felt the need to be good at riding. Like to survive, you needed to have the "right stuff."

This "right stuff" thinking was usually fine, and it helped spur on the hesitant or slightly lazy person to have a little more oomph when it came to improving one's self, but it could work in a detrimental way, if it became too pronounced on a person's list of priorities. In fact it could become an obsession. And an obsession could become a monster, and the monster could destroy what you were trying to accomplish in the first place. Roger and I had had a lot of help from God so far, out here in our new home, but the struggles weren't over. We were to have a struggle with the monster that I have just described. A struggle, and a hope, that with God, that monster in us could rise out of the ashes like the phoenix, but become something new and fresh and good.

We weren't living a fancy life out here in the valley, but it was a good life, even with its changeable weather, and more rustic living conditions than where we had come from. Walnut Creek was countryish, but nothing like this. It had sewers and natural gas. Out here, in addition to the common propane tank sitting in the back yard, we all had septic tanks, which occasionally rebelled against our toilets, making them retort back with low gurgling noises. They had an almost angry sound. I think maybe it sounded that way because of our conscience. Roger and I did carry some guilt along with us whenever the septic tank man had to come out and pump the tank, ever since Dad had labeled us the Toilet Paper King and Queen of Western Nevada. He wasn't trying to be mean, but to make a point. "Frugal with the paper in the toilet," he'd say, "generous with the paper in the basket." He meant for us to not use the toilet as a paper dump every time we killed a bug, or wiped our nose. Dad had become very emphatic with us, especially since the day he walked past the bathroom and saw Roger in there throwing paper towels into the toilet, that he had just used to wipe our cat Sniffy off with after giving him a sort of bath in the tub. It wasn't the standard bath, being more of a splashing than emersion, since Sniffy, like most people, was the antithesis of cooperation.

Lots were large, and neighbors sparser, than places in town. There were plenty of people raising their own steers to eat, even if they weren't ranchers, and some had horses or mules. Chickens and roosters could be heard in the early morning hours, with sheep and goats holding vigorous conversations, as the sun came up. There was only one hog farm that we knew of, and it seemed to be on its way out, with just a few pigs in small, low makeshift corrals that were becoming more dilapidated by the hour, and sagging with more broken boards than standing ones. Our parents loved it out here, and Roger and I, although still in transition mode from our move out of California suburbia, were appreciating it more as life went on.

There were, some days, however, that went against the flow of appreciation, and stuck out like a fly on a raspberry pop sickle. You wanted to eat and enjoy the cool sweetness on a hot day, but the fly...

In my life, on that particular day, Buck was the raspberry pop sickle, and Pearl 'Peachy' Blayne, was the fly. It just seemed as though she had been destined to be my tormentor.

"Hi Lissy!" Buck called, as he trotted up to me on Quick.

I was taking some library books out of our car in the front yard when Buck had come over with two other people on their horses. The sun was in my eyes, it being two o'clock, that Saturday afternoon, and very nice weather for this early spring like winter day.

"Hi Buck!" I called back.

Buck had been helping us a lot with Nevada Sage like Mr. Newman did. He came after school sometimes and every other weekend. Part of the time he would help his Dad with the cattle and alfalfa on his ranch towards the south end of the valley, but lately, he had been over at Mr. Newman's whenever he could. Sometimes he was over at the Blayne's house. I knew that he did work off and on for Mr. Blayne around his place, but I wondered how much he really enjoyed going over there to see Pearl. She really was attractive and had always shown so much interest in Buck. But at least I knew that he liked to do things with me too. We did go exploring the valley and taking pictures, which I would later do pen and ink drawings and watercolors from like he had suggested, and chasing rabbits with his dog 'Gyro.' At first we would take Smokey Blue, Mr. Newman's old horse, until his bad foot was just too bad to have any weight on it at all, even for a gentle little walk towards the Pine Nuts. So Mr. Newman let Buck keep his brown ranch horse, Quick, over at his place, for us to ride double on. Sometimes we would go with Roger and Nevada. The three of us had a great time. Roger thought Buck was the greatest thing since chicken in a basket, and Buck knew that I enjoyed being with him too. I was finally glad that we had moved to Carson Valley.

I stood there in my driveway squinting up at him, looking into his smiling face, with the warm brown hair and golden brown eyes that I had grown so fond of, framed by the dark brown cowboy hat and denim jacket that he always wore.

"Majesty! Quit!" I heard a girl's voice yell from one of the other horses. I shaded my eyes from the sun, and as the shadow of her big horse fell over me, I could see that the girl atop the mountainous bay steed, was none other than 'Peachy' Blayne. The horse, as he came more into focus to me, was gorgeous. His dark bay hair was almost black. He had three white socks and a streak of white on his black mane. His height was monumental. Well over fifteen and a half hands. Maybe over sixteen, I thought to myself in awe. Peachy's short blond hair and blue eyes were a harsh contrast against the dark steed. She looked out of them with a sharp steely glare, even though her mouth formed into a smile and emitted a halfway cordial greeting.

"Well hello there, little Lissy."

"Hi Pearl," I said, trying to be cheerful and look as old and dignified as I possibly could.

She sat atop her horse like a queen. Majesty moved his feet impatiently. She twirled him in a circle, scolded him again, then gave him a little pat on the neck. "Good boy," she said, like a condescending nursemaid. "He's a little hard for anyone to ride, but me. Dad likes me to take him out whenever I can. He needs a lot of exercise, being a warm-blood."

"Oh," I said. I didn't feel like putting myself out a lot to make a polite compliment about her beautiful horse, when she already acted like she was the 'noble princess' of the entire horse world.

The other rider said, "Peachy, let's go, it's getting late, and I want to get some riding in before the sun starts going down and it gets too cold. We may not even have enough time to ride much before spring if some more snow sets in. I can't believe such changeable weather..."

"Okay, Riva," she said to the other girl. "We need to get our practice in for the endurance anyway." Pearl turned to me again. "We're all going on practice endurance rides around Hot Springs Mountain, to get ready for the race that's coming up. Buck and I and Riva and her boy friend Bill, are going to be in it."

"It sounds like fun," I said.

Peachy got a twisted smile on her face again. "Well,

you have to be a good rider for this kind of thing. And you've got to have a GOOD horse. Little kids and little ponies don't make it in this kind of… "

"Pearl," Buck broke in, "Anybody can be in this race. It's open to all ages. The one by Fallon is a little harder to…"

"Well lets get going," she said back to Buck and Riva. She turned her head to Riva and said, "I'll race you!"

The two girls took off in flurry of dust and rocks grinding under their horses' feet. Pearl on her dark emperor, and Riva on her large red quarter horse-thoroughbred mix.

"Buck," I said. I was still sort of in shock. Steamrollered again, by Pearl Blayne. Why was she so mean to me? "What's going on? I asked him, trying to sound calm, but biting nails inside. "Are you really riding with those two?"

"Well, Pearl thinks I am, but I told her that I've got some work to do at home for the next three weeks. We're getting ready to move cattle from our winter pastures back up into the Pinenuts. I told her "maybe" I can. I've done some endurance riding before and thought it might be fun, but I hadn't planned on getting hooked up with a group especially."

"Oh," I said again, deadpan, like I had answered back to Pearl, with my lack of enthusiasm for the whole thing hanging out like a hound dog's tongue.

"Come on, Buck!" Pearl called from up the road. She and Riva had turned around and were walking their horses slowly back towards us. "Let's go!"

"Okay," he said.

"Lissy, I'll see you later. Grandpa said he's having your family over for a barbecue in a few days. He wants to get one in while the weather is halfway decent. He's hoping it'll snow again for a good water supply this year. I'll be back over for dinner then. I'll see you, okay? Bye Tulip!"

Buck had continued calling me Tulip, and I liked it. But I wasn't real happy with him today. Why did he put up with her, I wondered. Why didn't he just... oh I don't know... "Have a Peachy time with Peachy," I said under my breath. I closed the car door and walked toward the house. Why did I have to pick this time of day to get my library books out of the car? Now my whole life is changed.

12

Toenails and Marbles

It was Sunday. Roger dug to the bottom of the box in his closet looking for his good church shoes. He had found his black spider ring, a red bandana, and two golf balls under his old Teddy Bear blanket, but no shoes. He was almost resting on his head and had one leg stuck high up into the air behind him.

"Now where ARE those things," came his muffled voice from inside the box. "I get so tired of not being able to find my shoes! Mom! Mom! Come Here!" he ordered, still with his head inside the box. "I'm tired of this!" He waited for a minute, then lifted his head up and yelled at the top of his voice, "Mom!"

"For Heaven's sake, Roger," said Mom coming into his room. "What's the matter?" I wondered too, and peeked around her for a minute to see what was going on.

Dad had also come into the room right behind her. Before anybody could talk about shoes or finding things or say anything at all, he said very firmly to Roger, "I don't ever want to hear you talk to your mother that way again!"

"Sorry Dad," said Roger in a very quiet voice.

"Tell Mom that you're sorry. It's not your place to scold your mother, and she sure doesn't deserve to be treated that way."

"Sorry, Mom," he said. The bangs of his tan hair with the red lights in it fell over towards the side of his freckled face as he leaned down on his bent legs inside the big box like a dejected toad. He needs a haircut soon, I thought. I wish my hair color was as pretty as his. The little brat doesn't even appreciate it too.

Dad left the room while Roger kept his head down, pulling at a piece of frayed cardboard on the side of his box.

Mom told him, "We've got to go pretty soon, Roger. Maybe Lissy knows where your shoes are."

"Okay," he said. "I'll ask her."

Mom left, and I came into his room. He was still sitting there pulling at the box. I was in a hurry to get ready myself. I looked at him with irritation and said, "Okay Roger Muskrat, I don't know if I should help somebody so bratty or not, but what do you want?" I knew he was looking for his shoes but I wanted to make him grovel a little. Today I used my special Roger Muskrat name again, that I had given to him when he was a baby and his hair stuck up from the top of his head framing his dark brown eyes, reminding me of a little woodland animal that crawls in holes and plays games out in the dark at night. He had gladly accepted the title through the years without any problem, since he knew I meant it in an affectionate way. I called him that today, just to help myself be able to talk civil to him when he could be so irritating.

"Lissy, I know it's not right to talk BAD to Mom but a lot of kids talk the way I did to her.

"Who?" I said.

"Oh like the Journoir kids. I saw Henreid in the store with his mother last week and he talked that way to her. He was just being, I don't know the word, but he was trying to make his point to her."

"Emphatic?" I said.

"What?" he said.

"Emphatic. When you're trying to make a point with someone."

"Yeah, that's it."

"Well that's not emphatic. That's just being bratty and rude," I said. "And I can say that emphatically!"

"But I thought it was sort of all right to call Mom with a mad voice because I was frustrated," Roger said, in almost a baby voice. "I'm only ten, I mean, well nine, and I'll only be ten next, and she loves me, right? I thought she would understand. Why does Dad make such a big deal out of it?"

"Roger Muskrat," I said again, trying to retain remnants of any affectionate feeling that I had ever had for him. "A whine, she could accept. An obnoxious order coming from you like a drill sergeant, she won't. Do you see the difference?"

"Yeah, I guess so." He kept his head down, studying his feet inside the box. "Do you know where my shoes are?"

"You left them in the laundry room last night after Dad told you to pick up your marbles. Remember? You put them in your shoes and then set them on top of the drier. You didn't want to go all the way back to your room and miss part of the cartoon special that was on."

"So that's where my marbles are!" Roger said in surprise, "Why didn't anybody put them in my room for me?"

"Do you mean Mom and Dad and me? Roger, do you really think that we should put your things away for you?"

"Why not? You love me don't you?" He made a squirrelly little face when he said "love," and looked at me out of round little eyes that had sort of a 'stinky' look to them.

"Good grief Roger," I said. If you can't even put your stuff away and talk nice to Mom, how are you going to do other things right? The more you do right, the easier it is to do right. The more you do wrong, the easier it is to do wrong. I had no more patience that morning for him. "The bottom line is, Roger Muskrat... you need a brain adjustment."

I went around the corner into my room to get a necklace out of my jewelry box.

Roger called to me from his room. "Is that sort of like when Jerry Snellers used to brag that he could chew his toenails off like nothing, even though when he first tried to, it was hard because his leg was so stiff when he tried to get his toe up to his mouth? Because it is hard at first. But after a lot of times it gets easier. Is it like that Lissy!"

Okay, it was time to totally ignore him. "Mom," I said, as she walked by my room, "will you hook this necklace for me?"

"Sure," she said. It was a beautiful necklace – a crystal heart on a fourteen carat gold chain that my parents had given me for Christmas the last year we had been in Walnut Creek. I loved it, and it looked great with my plum sweater and skirt.

Mom looked nice in her brown and gold skirt and sweater. It went good with her brown hair and eyes.

"Mom," I said again, "Am I drab?"

"Drab?" she said. "What do you mean, "drab"?"

"Well, like colorless. Bleak. Boring."

"Of course not!" she said. You have beautiful skin, and shiny dark blond hair that sparkles when the sun shines on it, and very pretty eyes."

"My eyes are only green and brown, and my hair is so non-striking," I complained to her.

"Well, I don't know what you mean by "striking," but you're certainly not drab."

"Well I mean, I'm not real attractive like the older girls around here. Like… Pearl Blayne and her friend

Riva. Riva has long black hair and looks a little exotic like an actress or something, and Pearl is…"

"Pearl," Mom broke in, is a very pretty girl. The problem is, that she knows it. She could do with a little construction work on her inside pretty, if you know what I mean."

Everybody in our valley who knew her, would know what that means. She had developed a reputation of "the not very nice but extremely pretty girl" that I was afraid had been very attractive to just about every male soul in our area. I thought she must be a real challenge to the guys out here, or guys anywhere.

"Oh I know all that Mom, but I just feel so blah, next to her."

"Lisbeth Bloomingson, you listen to me! Is a tropical bird with colorful feathers beautiful? Like those big macaws that we saw on the nature channel last night."

"Well THEY are," I said gloomily.

"What about the deer that we saw back in Walnut Creek on our picnic up on Mt. Diablo?"

"Well they were real pretty, but…"

"Some people might call them drab, especially next to the macaws, but they really aren't are they? They have their own special kind of beauty. Sort of like Nevada. Some people think it's too dry and rugged, but we have seen some beautiful things out here haven't we? It has its own flavor. Just like people. They have their own flavor. We just need to not let our sin nature take over and make our flavor rotten. And that smells from the inside out."

"You mean like Pearl?" I said.

"I don't want to especially pick on Pearl, Lissy, because we all need to work on ourselves."

"Let's get moving," Dad called from the living room.

In less than one minute, we were out in the car. Even though the days were warm, we needed our coats to protect us from the morning chill. Roger and I sat next to each other in the back seat. "I'm cold," said Roger in a crabby voice.

"We'll warm up as soon as we get to church," Mom told him. The car heater was taking its time this morning, but sure enough, as soon as we entered the church building, our hands and noses began to thaw and mist up in the lights and the warmth. More people walked in behind us, and a flurry of coats and hats flew off of their owners to hang on the large gold hooks in the entry hall of the little Nevada church. I looked around for Buck and his family and Mr. Newman, then I remembered that they had all gone to Fallon to a relative's house for the day.

After Sunday School, the small congregation flocked into the sanctuary like eager birds ready to be fed with the Word of God. We would listen and learn, and some of us even, would carry these words out of church, to apply them to our everyday lives of laundry soap, feed bins, and cheese sandwiches.

The sermon today was a good one on "The Worst

Progressive Disease of Man". Roger and I could tell that it was good because of the up and down shaking heads on many of the adults around us. The minister was really getting through to them. But I noticed Roger didn't pay much attention himself. He was very busy sticking a paper clip into one of the offering envelopes, trying to make a hang glider that he had once seen an older boy at church do. And also, he felt obliged to look over at little Ricky Nard's turned head, two pews in front of him and to the right. Ricky was only seven, but he had a way of making the holes in his nose the largest that we had ever seen, while at the same time, stretching his tongue completely down the entire length of his chin in a tick-tock fashion. It reminded Roger and I of a piece of machinery we had seen on T.V. once, in a donut factory. To ignore those huge holes and tick-tocking tongue was unforgivable in seven-year-old society. Not to acknowledge it with a returned tick-tock was extremely rude. At the least impolite, or so Roger had told me at the time. To keep from laughing, I reminded myself how stupid it is to sink to the seven year old level like Roger is so ready to do. It's just so uncool.

"...and the first chapter of Romans, verses twenty-eight to thirty-two!" said the minister in a firm voice. "And even as they did not like to retain God in their knowledge, God gave them over to a reprobate mind, to do those things which are not convenient; Being filled with all unrighteousness, fornication, wickedness, covetousness, maliciousness; full of envy, murder, debate, deceit, malignity; whisperers, Backbiters, haters of God, despiteful, proud, boasters, inventors of evil things, disobedient to parents, Without understanding, covenantbreakers, without natural affection, implacable, unmerciful: Who knowing the judgment of God, that they which commit such things are worthy of death, not only do the same, but have pleasure in them that do them."

We listened to the Bible verses with a blurry mind, until verse thirty-two, when Roger returned a tick-tock to Ricky and made him laugh. His mother popped him on the head with her pencil and told him to turn around. We watched the back of Ricky's head and I could still picture the huge holes flexing in and out. I looked at Roger and had to stifle a giggle. He smiled at me. Mom touched Roger on the shoulder and quietly shook her head "no" to his tick-tocking. He sat back and folded his hands in his lap. Then he picked up the hang glider in progress and tried sticking the paper clip into it again. The minister, who was beginning to raise his voice, set his hand ever so firmly on the podium and said, "This is both the problem and the pattern, of sin. It will walk you down the pathway of life, like a dark cloaked figure attempting to put a blindfold on you, and eventually, one day, will succeed - if left unchecked..."

Despite the minister's good warning, I was so warm and cozy that my mind began to fade out to think only of Roger's lopsided hang glider, to Ricky's nose, to Roger's head bending to rest on Dad's shoulder. He must have been sleepy too...and soon the church service was over.

As we drove home from church along the highway, Dad said to us, "Look!" He pointed towards Mom's window in the front seat. We all looked in that direction. "Out there! Isn't he something!" It was a Red-tailed Hawk soaring above the grassy pasture next to the highway. The hawks came to the Carson Valley every winter during the cold months because of the milder weather in comparison to many places in the western United States. There were plenty of large fields for hunting mice and rabbits. One large rodent for breakfast and one for dinner would keep a bird that size just fine in a day.

The hawk flew, then glided, then seemed to rest on the wind for a minute. All of a sudden it shot downwards toward the field. It was exactly at the right spot, at the right time, because up it flew with a field mouse in its claws. The bird was so close to the car, that Roger and Mom, who were the nearest to it, could see it from underneath, clutching the mouse as it swung towards the right and flew off to settle in a large tree back down the road.

"What a fantastic bird! If only people were as determined to get rid of sin from their life as that hawk was to catch that mouse," said Dad to Mom.

I watched the hawk through the back window, while it soared off. I studied the bird with its flash of Mercurochrome red coloring around the tail feathers.

"Dad, I was talking to Roger this morning about doing little things right, so we can do bigger things right. Could we actually become wicked? What does God mean about people becoming more and more wicked? "Could we become more and more wicked? Will we ever have a blindfold on?"

"Lissy, God is talking about people who have rejected the knowledge of God that they have," said Dad. "Everyone, even people who are in a far off undeveloped place on earth have a basic knowledge of God."

"They do? Even in a jungle?" I sat up straight and leaned towards Dad so I could hear him better.

"King Kong would have been a nicer gorilla if he had been a Christian," blurted out Roger, sitting up next to me behind Dad.

"Roger…that is sooo…" I started to get mad because this was really important and I had been wondering about it for a long time, "That is soooo….stup…" I hesitated, and with closed eyes, squeezed out, "…annoying!"

Roger fell back onto the seat and pretended to be asleep. He started up his phony snoring.

Dad just ignored him. "That's right," he said. "God puts the awareness of Himself into people. They know that someone made everything. They know that THEY'RE here! They know that someone made them. They didn't create themselves."

"That would be kind of silly to think wouldn't it?" I said.

That's right, but people can get off on some strange

thinking that doesn't even make sense, when they reject God's truth. Some people here, in our country, have a lot of knowledge of God within themselves, and from without, and they still don't try to get right with Him. Even Christians can get on the track of repeated sinning, if they don't turn away from it. We all need to be careful."

"I think people are stranger than animals, sometimes," said Roger.

"I thought you were asleep," I said to him, still irritated.

"You just think I don't know what's going on all the time," said Roger.

"Well... I don't really know what you're thinking INSIDE your little scull... but from the OUTSIDE it looks pretty darn..." Mom gave me a funny look. "But anyway, Dad, what happens if they want to get right with God?"

"Well, God says draw near unto Him and He'll draw near unto you. He'll send more knowledge of Him when you seek it. The best thing He'll send is the Good News about Jesus dying for our sins, and believe me, His forgiveness is medicine to our soul."

I studied the back of his reddish brown hair for a minute. I knew that Dad knew what he was talking about. He had read the Bible for years. He had had a terrible time in the Korean War and wasn't just a bunch of blah blah about God. He had faith in Him, and he lived it.

Then people are able to accept Jesus as their Savior if they want to, I thought. I felt relieved. God wants us, I thought. He doesn't push us away. His forgiveness is medicine to our soul. I had no idea then how much medicine I would need from God that spring in Carson Valley. I leaned back into the seat and looked out at the sky for more hawks. I didn't see any, so I rested until the car brought us home.

13

Dinner at Mr. Newman's

Cowboy's Fried Egg

It was Tuesday night, and we headed over to Mr. Newman's for his barbecue. Buck was there. I was wearing my best pants and shirt, sort of a cowgirl flavored outfit - dark blue-gray levis, with a red plaid blouse with the cowboy pockets, and red lace around the collar and short sleeves. I hadn't cut my hair since leaving Walnut Creek, but now I usually wore it in a ponytail instead of braids. I didn't want to look too immature, but hadn't got to the point of the 'shag cut' that was becoming so popular, especially after hearing about Carol Barns.

I was in a good mood and looking forward to Mr. Newman's Texas style ribs. Mr. Newman was raised in Oklahoma but said, "The food was really good in Texas too!" We had had them before, and they were out of this world. Most of my good mood though, was spurred on because Buck would be there. We had such a good time together. We appreciated each other. We meshed.

"Howdy there, Bloomingson clan!" Mr. Newman greeted us at the back porch door. None of us ever bothered with our front doors. It wasn't necessary.

Our family was getting to know Mr. Newman pretty well. He was somewhere in his early sixties. He was an educated man. He was born in Oklahoma to part Cherokee parents and had come out to Nevada as a young man. His education was in mining and ranching. He wasn't wealthy, but he had done all right, and was generous and helpful to his neighbors. While slightly overweight, with a medium build, he had a handsome demeanor and carried himself well, despite a slight limp from arthritis from an old leg injury. He was a man of great faith in God, and our family was glad to have him as a neighbor and friend. Roger and I liked him.

His house was real interesting to us. It was full of cowboy stuff. Some decor, and some real artifacts from the ranch he used to own in Fallon, that he had passed on to his son. There were cast iron frying pans of various shapes and sizes, branding irons, rusted over blacksmith equipment from the 1800's and some very old cowboy toys in cases. It was like a museum, and every time we went over there, I noticed something new.

"Hey Lissy," said Buck from inside the house. "Come here, I want to show you something."

"Okay," I called. I went into the dining room and looked on the table. There was a large blown up photo of a horse and Buck's black and white Border Collie, Gyroscope. They were touching noses. The horse was standing with his head pointed towards the ground, and Gyro on his hind legs with his nose almost in the horse's teeth.

"That's Mickey with Gyro," said Buck. He looked at the photo with a fond but professional look. I knew he was sort of proud of the photo. At least very satisfied with the results. It was a very good shot. The background tack room and trees added to the picture, as if someone had designed a set.

"Oh it's great!" I said. "What a neat picture! Gyro is such a funny dog, even though he's really pretty!"

"He really is some dog," said Buck. "Some of the things that he does are pretty wild!"

We laughed and talked about Gyro for quite a while, and Buck told me the story about Mickey and how they had got him from an old roping champion. I noticed that Buck was wearing a new looking green plaid shirt with cowboy pockets. His hair had grown out some and I could see what a pretty brown it was next to the various greens in his shirt. He was probably totally unaware of how it looked pretty on him, being a guy and all, and probably would never care, but at least he had bothered to put on something nice for tonight. That was a good sign to me.

"Oh what's this picture here?" I asked. "It looks like that pretty flower that's in our yard, and I see them in the hills here and there. It's really neat too!"

"I forget what the real name is," said Buck, "but around here we call them, 'Cowboy's fried eggs."

"Wow. They sort of look like it!" I said.

"All aboard the rib train," said Mr. Newman. They were ready, and it was time to eat.

Mr. Newman asked the blessing on our food, and we all dove into the buffet style ranch dinner with pinto beans, 'tater' salad, fried okra and cornbread on the side. I had just got through three fourths of my first mouth-watering rib, when the doorbell rang.

"I'll get it Grandpa," said Buck as he jumped up from the table and quickly wiped his hands.

"Oh hi there…" I heard Buck say in quiet surprise as he opened the door. "Uh. . ...come on in, Pearl."

PEARL? PEARL? The fly on the Popsicle Pearl? Not at my barbecue with Buck!

"I'm sorry to bother everybody," she said as she came towards the dining room in a swift little walk. She had on a soft fuzzy powder blue sweater with black pants and small silver earrings with light blue stones. "I just didn't know what to do," she continued in her sweetest friendliness. My mare Misty is acting sort of funny like she doesn't feel good and Majesty is acting upset too.

118

I just don't know what to think! I wondered if I could have a little help for just a minute or two? Dad's out of town until tomorrow."

"Well I'll be glad to come over and have a look," said Mr. Newman. He knew, as we were learning too, that ignoring a sick horse was not on the safety zone map of horsemanship. They could colic and get bound up or twisted before you realized what was happening and be dead by the next morning.

"Well that's okay, Mr. Newman," said Pearl quickly. "I don't want to take you away from your company. I mean that would be terrible, you having a barbecue and all. I was thinking that maybe if I could just borrow Buck for a minute... ?"

"Oh," said Mr. Newman. He had got half-way up for a second, ready to help Pearl in what we all had believed to be a real emergency, but had sat back down with a funny look in his eyes, and his mouth was a little scrunched up. "Okay, sure. You want to see what you can do Buck?" he said without a lot of emotion.

"Well, uh... sure, Grandpa. I guess." He looked around at us quickly, "I'll be back in a few minutes. I don't want to miss out on those ribs. They're great!"

"She's mighty dressed up for horse doctoring," Mr. Newman said quietly to Mom and Dad after Buck left with Pearl.

Mom and Dad and Roger all agreed that the ribs were great, but I just sat there like a pot of pudding making the first little bubbles when it starts to boil.

"Lissy pass the pepper PLEASE," said Roger happily. "I want to put some on my 'tater' salad. It's good!"

"Well, thanks Roger," said Mr. Newman. "It's a special recipe of my wife Edna. Sure wish she was still on earth here to make it for us instead of me. She did a much better job!"

"You did a good job, Mr. Newman!" said Roger.

"You sure did," said Mom. "I might even try to wiggle the recipe out of you one day!"

"Sure thing," said Mr. Newman. "Then I could come to your house and eat it. It would probably be better than mine, anyway."

Everybody laughed and enjoyed eating and talking for quite a while. I was only half there, trying to smile and be pleasant. Where were they? Did Buck have to be gone this long? What kind of plans did Pearl have up her sleeve now? Sick horse? I really wondered.

After more than an hour had gone by, Mr. Newman looked at his watch and said," I wonder what's going on with the sick horse." He looked at Mom and Dad.

Dad said, "Do you think they need any help?"

"I think Buck would call us if they did." He and Dad looked at each other. They kind of stared as if they wanted to shake their heads, but thought it was better not to.

I was disappointed and angry. I knew that Pearl 'Peachy' Blayne had devised an 'emergency' at just the right time. The right time for her. This was it, I thought. This was just 'it.' I was going to take action. Action against 'the fly.' But what?

I thought about that until we went home. I could barely say good-bye to Mr. Newman and thank him for dinner in the proper way because I was so distracted.

"I'm sorry Buck had to leave, Lissy," Mr. Newman said as we were going out the door. "It was probably a little boring for you tonight."

"That's okay, Mr. Newman," I said. But I think he knew that I felt bad. He seemed to know things about people.

We had barely got inside our back door, when I got Mom aside and began whining to her. "Can you believe it Mom? How she came and got Buck out of there away from"...I hesitated a minute... "from US!"

"Well I'm not positive that she didn't have a sick horse," said Mom, "but it did seem a little strange the way it all happened tonight..."

"STRANGE!" I said. "I think it was terrible, just terrible!"

I began to cloud up and start into the whine-cry mode when Mom stopped in the middle of our hallway and said, "Lissy Bloomingson, why are you always so worried about Pearl? She's not really that important in your life. You and Buck are good friends, and I don't think you have to be so concerned about her."

"But why does she act that way when she's so good looking? Why does she have to push me down below her all the time? Every chance she gets, she tries to make me look stupid. If she was pretty and NICE, then

121

I would probably admire her and try to be like her, but she's so awful. She makes me sick!"

"I don't know why she's like that Lissy. A lot of people are atrocious to other people. From beggars to kings, there are people who inflict evil on others. People have a sin nature, and they're always having an inner battle with evil behavior. It's the ones that don't put up a fight against it that are really destructive to other people."

"Well Pearl Blayne is just about the most... "

"Lissy, you need to ask God to help you with this and not stew. Now get ready for bed. We're all turning in early - school tomorrow."

I went to my room. The theology of cruel unrighteousness in people didn't help me a lot tonight. I was still in my own little dither about things... I really should get my driver's license, I thought. That would make me look a lot older. And I would feel a lot older too. Why had I been such a chicken about it? I had lagged getting my driver's permit until I was almost sixteen. And I was still lagging! Now the delay was really turning on me in a bad way. That'll take time, though, to be driving. I'll need a little more practice, then all the tests and stuff. What can I do now? What can I do now... Wait a minute! I know! It's about horses! I know what to do! I'll ask Dad tomorrow. That's what I'll do! I'll ask Dad tomorrow. The Peachy Blaynes of this world may push most people down, but not me. I was going to rise up out of this mud bog of misery myself. In my own way. I'll ask Dad tomorrow!

14

At The Feed Store

I got up early the next day. I wanted to catch Dad before he left for work. I hadn't realized that he was leaving even earlier today.

"Where's Dad?" I said to Mom as I shuffled into the kitchen in my bathrobe and house shoes.

"He's headed for work. I think he left. Oh maybe he's still in the front yard."

"Oh no!" I said. I ran to the front door and opened it with a little crash against the small entryway hall. It swung back towards my elbow and I pushed it out of the way with a second little crash.

"Careful Lissy!" Mom called from the kitchen.

"Oh, sorry!" I yelled. "Dad! Dad! Wait!"

He was inside his Ford pickup and had just started the engine.

"What's the matter Lissy Girl!" he called cheerfully.

Good. He looked in a good mood.

"Dad," I said. He looked at me.

"What?" he said.

"Dad. You know how I enjoy Roger's horse, and we've talked about getting me one too if I want one. Well, I want one."

"Okay," he said. "I think it would be great if you and Roger could go riding together. We'd let him go a little farther if he wasn't alone."

"Oh good," I said. "Thank you Dad!"

"Okay, well I've got to leave now. We'll talk more about it when I get home. Mr. Newman said he would help us find you a good horse. I'll see if he's free one of these coming weekends to go with us if there's a horse to look at."

"But that's going to take so long! Can't we…"

"Lissy I'll talk to you when I get home."

"Okay," I said. I guess I should let Dad go to work, and not start annoying him, I thought.

He rolled up the widow and waved at me with a little smile. I waved back. I've got to keep my cool, I told myself, and not turn into a nut about it.

That day after school, my new friend JoAnna, who lived about a half mile away from us, was being picked up by her Mother. Mom said I could ride home with them.

"I've got to stop by the feed store on the way home," said Mrs. Amile. "We're out of scratch for the chickens, and I need some hay for the goats."

The feed store, I thought. Good that'll be fun. Maybe they'll have some puppies or kittens in there today.

It was a large place. Like a big metal barn. There were rows of animal supplies. Brushes, combs, biscuits, halters, ropes, dog, cat and horse shampoos, worm paste medicine for horses, and hoof remedies. Almost everything you could think of. It smelled of sweet grains and animal medicine. I liked it. It was a friendly place with two women and one man that seemed to know their products forward and backward.

"I'm getting a horse," I told JoAnna.

"Really, Lissy?" she said. "That's pretty neat. Do you know what kind yet?"

"Not yet," I said. "But something big, I hope." I surprised myself. I had wanted a standard size horse in the past, and I was getting excited about being able to ride with Roger, and especially with Buck, but ever since the last 'Peachy' incident, I had started thinking 'BIG' and 'IMPRESSIVE."

"What's this?" said JoAnna. She was looking at a bulletin board on the wall near the cash register. "Appaloosa mare for sale. Broke to Ride. Good price. Inquire at cash register."

"A horse for sale," I said thoughtfully, not really to anyone, mostly to myself.

"Are you going to ask about it Lissy?" said JoAnna.

"I don't know. I guess so."

One of the feed store ladies came back behind the desk and was ringing up a purchase for a customer. When she was done, I asked her, "Excuse me, there's a sign there about a horse. An Appaloosa…"

"Oh she belongs to Gerdie out in the back. She's out loading hay, but you can go back and talk to her if you want to."

"Okay," I said. "Thank you."

JoAnna and I walked to the back of the store, and went into an even larger storage area full of alfalfa, grass hay, and large feed supplement sacks. There was a husky shouldered girl with short strawberry blond hair pulling hay bales onto a customer's pick-up with hay hooks in her hands. She was thin, but pretty strong for a girl.

"Excuse me," I said. "Do you have a horse for sale?"

"Horse for sale," she said, as she wiped her forehead with her arm. "Oh that's right. You saw my sign, right?"

"Right," I said.

"You ride?" she said.

"Uh, yeah, I do. My brother has a horse."

"Good," she said. "Whatcha lookin' for?"

"Oh, something good size."

"Well," she said, "We've got that Appy mare that you saw on the sign. We're getting some new stock, and we'd like to sell a few horses before we bring more in. Got too many. I was going to trailer her over to my friends place tomorrow to stay, but I could bring her to your place instead. She's thirteen, stout, and she's a pretty easy keeper."

"What does she look like?" I asked.

"Oh she's a picture," the girl said. You can see her coming a mile away. She's a red Appy. Very striking.

She's really pretty when she sheds out in the summer."

Striking. A striking horse. It sounded pretty good, I thought. And she could bring her over tomorrow.

"Okay," I said. At least I thought it would be okay. "Oh wait a minute," I said. "How much is she?"

"Five hundred dollars," the girl said. "You could take a look at her when I bring her over."

"Okay," I said again. I gave her my address, but didn't think to give her my phone number, or get hers.

"Wow, it looks like you just made a horse deal," said JoAnna with admiration as we walked toward the car. As I thought of how I had done all that business deal talking that day, I admired myself a little too.

When I got home, I ran into the house to tell Mom the exciting news.

"What?" she said. "Lissy, you should have waited for Dad to be with you while you pick out a horse. Mr. Newman would go with you too, to help you pick out the right kind." Since Mom had ridden horses as a girl, she knew more than I had realized in the past, but I sure didn't want to hear about what she knew, today.

"But you'll like her Mom. She's an easy keeper, she's stout, she's real pretty when she sheds out in the summer, and she's STRIKING!"

"Lissy, I don't know…"

"Mom, can't we just look at her! She's bringing her over tomorrow."

"Tomorrow? Lissy, Dad called me today and said he won't be home until tomorrow evening. He's staying overnight in Fallon. He has to have another meeting with a customer tomorrow and doesn't want to drive home and have to go right back. And I'm picking up Mrs. Dibbs and taking her to town to get her car from the brake shop tomorrow afternoon. You picked a bad day for horse trading."

"But I'll be here, Mom. You want me to stay with Roger anyway, don't you? I'll take care of all the horse stuff. You should have seen me in the feed store. JoAnna thought I did a pretty good job."

"A good job of what?"

"Of horse trading," I said.

"Lissy, you'll have to call that girl and tell her not to bring the horse out until Dad gets home."

"I can't. I don't have her phone number."

Mom looked weary and angry. "Right now, I'm fixing dinner. I'll talk to you later about this."

"Okay," I said quietly. "Uh… I'll set the table for you in a few minutes."

I went to put my school things away, so I could go wash my hands before setting the table. Why did Mom have to overdo it on all the worrying stuff about the right kind of horse, and waiting until the right time. I needed a good, big horse to be able to ride with Buck and Pearl in the endurance practice NOW. If I waited for all that other stuff, I'd never get anything done!

15

Haley Roo

Roger wasn't feeling good that night, so Mom was pretty taken up with checking his temperature, and bringing him Pepsi water with a straw, and asking him what he had eaten during the day. After some prodding, she found out that he had had numerous cookies with some apple chunks over at Bradley's house, who lived on the two acres behind us. We had wondered why he didn't want to eat his hot dogs and beans tonight, that he usually loved, and always swept up off his plate like a little suckerfish sweeps off the bottom of the fish tank.

"They're not Kosher," he had said, sitting at the table with his eyes in droopy slits, trying to act like there was something wrong with the hot dogs, and everyone else around him, instead of letting the truth out that he was full of cookies and apple chunks.

"Well it just so happens, that they are," said Mom, "and they're very good hot dogs too."

"Well I want a bun," he said with dignified mal-content. He had already asked about buns before dinner, and Mom had said we were out of them. Boy, what's under HIS saddle, I wondered that night. Mom couldn't figure it out either until she sent him to bed after he complained of feeling sick, and then started asking him questions.

"Roger, what did you eat today?" she had asked him. "What did you have at Bradley's house?"

"Well, just some stuff," he said with a yawn.

"What stuff?" she said, pinning him down.

"Some apple chunks…and just some cookies."

"What kind of cookies?" Mom said, closing in on the kill.

"Oh, just some Oreos… and some apple raisin cookies… and some fig bars, and a few, well you know, real little chocolate snaps. They're real flat," he said, as if that would make up for the other 'thicker' cookies.

"Oh boy," said Mom. "And fig bars too." She shook her head.

We all went to bed tired. I had to finish a book report, and put clean sheets on my bed. Mom was tired from Roger, and as I look back on it, probably from me too. We didn't talk anymore about the horse that night. Surely this would work out. I was actually excited for tomorrow to come.

And tomorrow did come, and with it, the horse that I had so neatly bargained for was to come too. There was no way to stop it. Surely it would work out.

Roger was okay in the morning, so we both went to

school. Mom got a phone call from Mrs. Dibbs as we were leaving for the bus, and she said, "Remember, I'm taking Mrs. Dibbs to town this afternoon. Dad won't be home until tonight, so be sure to stay here with Roger, Lissy!"

"Okay Mom," I called.

JoAnna and I met at lunch in the cafeteria like we usually did on cooler days.

Sometimes Buck would look for me and eat with us, but most of the time he would go off with 'the guys' and fool around on the basketball courts, either inside or outside depending on the weather. The temperature had taken a dive last night. It had looked like snow, but to everyone's surprise, the weather channel changed its whole story this morning and predicted a warm spell again. Nobody seemed to know what the weather was doing. We hadn't had enough snowy months this year. Concerns for drought were now in the air.

"Wow, these concerns of adults never end, do they?" I said haughtily." I was in a good mood that day.

"The warm weather that's coming will be good to ride your new horse in, won't it?" said JoAnna with almost as much enthusiasm as I had.

"That's right," I said. "It's a good thing…"

"You got a horse?" said Malcome Myers, who was sitting across the table from us.

"Well not yet, but I'm getting one."

Malcome, who was from the Roaming T ranch family out here, was a blunt sort of person. Not a stupid person. He seemed to know some things, but he was just sort of irritating because he was so blunt.

"What are you getting?" he said.

"An Appaloosa mare."

"Who from?"

"Uh, Gerdie, I can't remember her last name."

A little smile began to creep up on Malcome's face. "Light red hair and muscles?" he said.

"Yeah, I guess so," I said.

"Not Gerdie! You're buying an Appy horse from Gerdie?" He began to laugh. "Oh boy…" he said. The bell rang. He jumped up to go.

"Wait a minute," I said. "What's so funny?"

"You'll find out!" he said as he walked away.

"Now what did he mean by that?" I said to JoAnna.

"Oh nothing probably. He just likes to act like he knows everything." JoAnna looked after him with a lot of interest on her face. I could tell she kind of liked him and disliked him at the same time.

"These ranch guys know a lot about horses, don't they?" I said to her.

"I guess they know a lot, but they want you to think that they know EVERYTHING!" she said with her head swinging around in a circle.

I hoped that was true - that Malcome didn't know everything and could be wrong or stupid or confused or something. I hoped that all the way home.

When I got off of the bus, I saw something down the road in front of our driveway. It was a tan horse trailer behind a red truck. I started running. She must be here! The horse must be here!

When I got to our yard and started to catch my breath a little, I looked around to the back of the trailer. On the top of the wheel well, Gerdie was sitting in the shade under our olive tree smoking a cigarette. Being nineteen, she was old enough to smoke, but it was the WAY she talked and looked and smoked that made her look like one very tough little cookie.

"Hey!" she said as she saw me.

"Hi!" I said.

"Back out of the way there a little," she said, "while I open the trailer up here," with the cigarette still hanging out of her mouth.

"What you have here, is the best of the breed," she said. "She's got a lot of the 'old world' Appaloosa in her. Good hindquarters. Good feet."

A high-pitched squeal suddenly emitted from inside the trailer, and those four good feet began pounding the inside of the trailer stall.

"Ho, girl!" said Gerdie. "Easy there!"

I took a couple of steps backward. The tailgate was down. Within two seconds, 1200 pounds of agitated Appaloosa was standing by my driveway underneath our olive tree. She was looking at me with dark brown eyes popped out of whitish pink rims that looked like they had just exploded into two little balls from the inside of a white and dark chocolate factory.

"She looks a little upset," I said in near disbelief, that

anything domesticated could look so wild. She really was pretty, even though her fuzzy winter coat was still pretty thick. And she WAS striking. She had a sorrel, or more of a burnt orange head and neck, with white flecks, and a white rump with large spots of the same orange-brown covering it.

I hoped I would be able to ride her okay. It would be a lot of fun to be on such a magnificent animal, next to the other horses on the endurance trail.

"Now I'll leave her here today," said Gerdie. "It'll help me out, and you can get used to her. I'll come by either tonight or tomorrow to settle up with you. I've got a lot to do, getting set up for the new stock. Got to redo some cross fencing before we have horses comin' outa our ears. Here's her other halter, in case you need it."

"Thanks," I said. I looked down at the halter and saw some metal plates in a bronze color, screwed into the side of the black halter strap. "What does this mean?" I read out loud, "Hâlé Roux."

"Oh that's the fancy French name for her. It means, I think, sunburned, or sun burnt red." She took a last puff on her cigarette, then threw it on the ground and squashed it with her foot.

"Really," I said. A fancy French name, I thought to myself. A name to stand up to 'Mr. Majesty.' Actually I had nothing against HIM. It was his owner that I had antagonism toward.

"But we don't call her that," continued Gerdie. "We

call her 'Haley Roo."

"Oh," I said. "Haley Roo." Well I guess that's okay, I thought.

Gerdie brought her into our back pasture and unhooked the lead rope. Nevada Sage had been running around making a ruckus the whole time we were in the front yard. He knew there was another horse out there. He and Haley Roo ran towards each other. They stopped with noses just barely touching, sniffed a long horse greeting, squealed, then stood there standing next to each other in the pasture like they had been acquainted for years.

A few minutes later, Roger got off the bus, and came running into the backyard after seeing the horse trailer pulling away.

"What's going on!" he said. "Wow, who's that!"

"That," I said, "is Haley Roo."

"What?" said Roger. "What's a Haley Roo?"

"It's a sun burnt red horse," I told him, like a teacher talking to a pupil.

Roger walked up closer to look at her. "Wow, he makes Nevada look almost little."

"He's a she," I said.

Roger just looked at me. I started to feel a little warm. Why was I nervous? I would try to look at things in a calm and rational way.

"She looks like a real bombshell to me," he said matter-of-factly.

What did my little brother know about things like

this! How could he know if she's a bombshell or not? My little brother!

"Roger," I said, "She's just fine. She's just nervous because she's new here."

"Well let's go pet her then," he said.

"Let's do that later. I haven't even been in the house yet."

"Okay," he said.

Good. He's not going to argue and act like he's Hoppalong Cassidy and my horse trainer, all rolled into one.

We went into the house, and I looked out the window over the kitchen sink at Haley Roo. She was standing next to Nevada calmly, but staring at the house, and at me through the window. She knew I was looking at her. Almost without a conscience effort, my mind reeled out a sentence, ' I wonder what plans she has for me.' I looked back at her for a minute, then went to my room to put my school things away.

Mom and Dad got home that evening at almost the same time. Mom got home first, but she didn't notice Haley Roo out in the pasture. It was getting dark later now. I hoped that Mom wouldn't look out the window while she was putting food on the table for a 'quickie' dinner to be ready for when Dad got there.

I had run out to give some hay to Nevada and Haley Roo, just before Mom got home. Roger had been busy at the bathroom sink, putting water into various kinds of paper bags. Someone had told him a joke at school about bringing your soup home from a restaurant in a doggie bag, and he wanted to check "scientifically" to see if it was possible. I was glad he was occupied then, because I knew as soon as I let him, he would be out there all over Haley Roo, driving her and me both, nuts.

"Dad called me from Silver Springs, so he should be home soon," Mom said to me, while breaking up lettuce chunks. "Will you turn that burner down a little for me please, Lissy?"

"Okay," I said. "Mom. Uh, you know that h…"

"Oh, I forgot to bring in the milk from the car!" said Mom. "Will you go get that for me please, Lissy? Roger, get washed up, it's almost time to eat!"

"O… Okay," I said. I started to get more nervous about breaking the news to Mom and Dad about our new addition. Should I tell them both when Dad's home? Should I just take them out there and show them? I had a feeling this wasn't going to be as simple as I had hoped.

Dad got home, and since everybody else was starving, we sat down at the dinner table as soon as possible. I wasn't that hungry, but I did take some salad and a roll. Then I passed them on to Roger, when we heard a funny noise out in the back pasture.

"What's that?" said Roger.

I looked at him with a glare that could cut ice, but the little oaf didn't even pay attention.

"Oh, I know what it is," he said. "Did Lissy tell you

about..."

"Roger, let me tell them."

A huge squeal came from the pasture, and the large metal feed bin that I had fed the horses in that night sounded like it was breaking in half. "What IS that!" said Mom.

"I don't know," said Dad, "but we better go out and look."

We turned on the outside light and walked out to the pasture fence. There was Nevada over in the left front corner of our pasture by himself, shaking a little, and looking pretty nervous and forlorn. Haley Roo was standing in a large pile of scattered hay with her two front feet inside of the feed bin that was now laying on its side.

"What in the world is that?" asked Dad.

"That's Haley Roo," I said. "My new horse."

16

Dismay and Trepidation

I was glad that it was today. I was even more glad that it wasn't last night anymore. At first I thought Dad would never speak to me again, and Mom would probably not let me eat at the dinner table with normal people. But after all the initial bawling out and the "Lissy Bloomingsons!" were said, I felt I would probably live again, no matter how miserable the ensuing days would be. We had no way to contact Gerdie, and I didn't hear just a little about that either. I began to realize that I had blown it big-time, and wasn't the cracker-jack horse trader that I had esteemed myself to be. What else could go wrong, I wondered.

Dad talked to Mr. Newman the next morning about what had happened. I think Dad didn't exactly know what to do. He probably needed advice, and also a little moral support. It was such a goofy situation that I had put us all in. Mr. Newman agreed that 'the older girl' should never have tried to do a horse deal with a 'an inexperienced teenager' which didn't make me feel a whole lot better, but he had told Dad and I, "Well now, no need to panic. I'll have a look at her with you today when I get back from the farm bureau, and Lissy's home from school. Just make sure that you feed them separately. One of them will have to be locked in the small pipe corral while they eat, because that mare won't let your little guy get his proper nourishment, and she'll overeat on his food."

"Thanks a lot, Sam," Dad said.

I could hardly wait for 3:40 to come, when I would be home to see what would happen about Haley Roo. Was there hope after all, that I would be able to keep her?

"Hi Mom!" I said. "Is Dad coming home early today?"

"He should be," she said.

"Are you still horribly mad at me?" I asked her.

"Well I would be, if I had never made any mistakes in my life before." She smiled at me. "I just hope you've learned something from this."

"Oh I have! I have," I said, flying out the back door. I had no idea at the time, just how much more I was going to learn.

"Okay, Haley Roo," I said to the big mare, as I went through the smaller pasture gate from our backyard, "Let's have some fun."

I kept talking to her in a friendly way as I walked towards her. She was new here, and I understood that. I would feel a little nervous if I was her…but now, what in the world was she doing? She turned her back to me and started walking away. I walked after her. She turned around and went in a circle. I circled. She circled again. This went on for it seemed like, too long for anything that had a brain, and a will to be cordial with another life form, to continue. I realized after my feet were sore from going back and forth in the sandy dirt, and wiping a little dust from my eyes, that Haley Roo, did not want to be caught.

Mr. Newman hollered over to me through his back window, "I'll be over in a few minutes Lissy, as soon as I get off the phone!"

"Okay Mr. Newman. Thanks!"

I went inside to get a drink of water. Roger was home from school. He was in deep conversation with Mom about the Journoir boys. Good. He probably hadn't seen me out in the pasture today walking in circles behind Haley Roo's hind end.

The Journoir boys had come down to ride their bikes in front of our house again, and they were just about the most exciting kids that Roger had ever had the honor to play with - or so he thought then. They had, a few days ago, to his surprise, invited him over to spend Saturday with them.

There were four of them. Derek, Damon, Henreid, and 'Babs' - all brown-eyed brown-haired stair steps, except for the youngest, Babs, who had more of a sandy colored head, but with the same intense and determined dark brown eyes as the rest of them.

The other day, when the boys had been in front of

our house, Henreid, who was in Roger's class, claimed that it was his idea to invite Roger over, until Damon, who was three years older than Henreid, lifted his arm into the air and gave him a sharp slap on the top of his head saying, "It was my idea, you dummy!"

Roger had cringed when he told us about it, and said he thought it was a pretty rough thing for Damon to do to Henreid, but the boys kept on playing and riding and yelling and having such a good time that Roger said he thought they were really 'okay' guys, even if they were kind of rough with each other.

Today, Derek, the oldest of the boys, and the most aloof, waved his brothers on towards home saying that he was hungry, and that they had all better get moving, or else.

Roger yelled good-bye a few times and stood watching them ride away like a wolf pack on a hunt. He talked about what great guys they were and how neat it must be for the four of them to be together. The four of them always having fun. They didn't seem to have to check in with their mother like he did all the time. Henreid bragged about NEVER having to keep his room clean. "It's a mess!" he'd yell in ecstasy. "I love it!" When the teacher collected homework assignments, Henreid hardly ever turned his in. Roger knew that, because he sat right next to him and he always wondered why or how Henreid could get away with that, without anything bad ever happening to him.

Derek and Damon pretty much blended in at school, except for something Roger had heard once about

Derek. Something about a tool missing from the custodian's supply room. Someone had seen him walking out of it the day that it was first missing, but nothing had really happened about it and we figured the whole thing must have blown over. So Roger was pretty much on top of the world when he came into the house that afternoon and asked Mom if he could spend the day Saturday with the Journoir boys.

"Did their mother invite you?" was the first thing that she asked Roger. I could tell he had known that she would ask that.

"I think so," he said in irritation. "I guess that's why they could ask me." He looked at her with a frown.

"Roger, I'm not trying to upset you, I'm just making sure that it's okay for you to go. Where do they live?"

"At the end of our street," said Roger, still very irritated. "Only way up towards the hills. Derek, that's Henreid's big brother, says that it's about three fourths of a mile from here. I have so much fun with them Mom. Can I go? Pleeeeese!"

"I'll have to call their Mom and make sure. And talk to Dad. We'll see."

"We'll see? We'll see?" he said. "What do you mean 'we'll see'? It's Saturday that I have to go up there. I need to know now!"

Dad walked into the house and came into the kitchen where we were. "What's going on here Katy?" he said to Mom. "Roger, aren't you talking a little louder than necessary?"

He could tell that Dad didn't hear the whole thing and didn't know just how loud and rude he had been.

"Roger asked me if he could go to the Journoir's place Saturday to spend the day. I guess I should call their mother tonight to make sure that it's all right. What do you think? I've done volunteer work with Mrs. Journoir at school a few times and they came once to our church around Christmas time. She seems like a nice person and I enjoyed talking with her."

"I don't see why not," said Dad, after he picked up a screwdriver off of the counter, and was tapping it on his thumbnail lightly. He was giving Roger the same kind of look that he gave to the roses in the backyard along the fence when searching for aphids and spider mites.

Roger seemed quietly glad but didn't look as happy as I thought he should have. He went to his room to play while Mom phoned Mrs. Journoir.

"Hello? Mrs. Journoir? Hi. I'm Katy Bloomingson. Roger's Mom. He's in Henreid's class at school. Yes, we helped with the Christmas play and the Valentine's Day party together. Yes...well, I'm fine. I, uh...well your boys, I guess, have asked Roger over for the day Saturday? Yes. I guess so.... oh...oh you didn't know about it?"

Roger peeked his head around the corner of the kitchen.

"Oh dear," Mom continued. "Well then, we won't... oh. It's fine with you? Yes, I like to have my kids have someone to play with too. Well, okay. We'll watch him go up the street until he meets your boys. Saturday at ten o'clock? Fine. When he comes home, his dad will meet him up the street in the afternoon before dinner then. Great! Thank you! Bye."

"Oh I get to go! I'm so glad! Boy, and they didn't even have to ask their mother first. She just said yes anyway. She sure must be nice."

Mom looked sort of bothered by that all evening, even after she had talked to Roger about how kids should get permission from their parents first about doing things with other kids. She said when she had seen Mrs. Journoir at school and at church, that she was an attractive woman with light hair and hazel eyes, slightly on the dainty side, and that she had always looked a little bit sad.

Mr. Newman was out in our backyard. Dad gave Mom a quick kiss, and went outside into the backyard with me. Roger followed us.

"I saw you had a little trouble cozying up to her!" Mr. Newman said to me.

"I couldn't get close to her at all."

"That happens sometimes," he said. "Try it again right now."

"Okay," I said.

I walked back out into the pasture and started the same routine.

"Hi, Haley Roo," I said.

She turned around again, with her rump towards me, and walked away. Mr. Newman had given me the lead rope, so I could hook it onto her halter. I circled around her to her front. She circled. I circled. She circled, and I circled again.

"Okay," said Mr. Newman. "C'mon back here."

He took the rope from me and said, "Wait here." He swung the rope around his head in the air and walked towards her. She took off like a shot and circled our fenced in pasture area at top speed. Dad and Roger and I stayed close by the fence. Mr. Newman walked around in a small circle in the middle of the pasture swinging the rope. He did that for a while, until Haley Roo looked like she was slowing down a little. Finally, she stopped. Mr. Newman looked straight at her and walked towards her with the rope down by his side. When he got up to her, she turned around again, with her rump towards him, and walked away. He swung the rope up over his head, and had her traveling in circles around the pasture again. She slowed down again, stopped, and looked at him. He walked towards her. She turned around again, with her rump towards him, and walked away. He circled her around the pasture again, and again she turned her back on him. He walked back to us at the front of the pasture and said. "Do you have some grain?"

Dad said, "We have some oat molasses, don't we Lissy?"

"I'll go get it," I said.

I could hear Mr. Newman talking to Dad while I was in the tack room.

"She looks like she might be a tough one. She's thir-

146

teen years old. If she was a foal, or real green, you might expect this, but I have a funny feeling about her."

"I do too," said Roger.

I could just bust Roger, I thought, as I handed the grain to Mr. Newman.

"Well let's catch her with this," he said. "Lissy you hold this bucket and shake it while we walk towards her. It's hard for horses to resist the smell of that grain."

He was right. In fact, she started walking up to us even before we got halfway over to her, and even before I started shaking the grain bucket.

"She knows already," I said to Mr. Newman.

"I think she knew yesterday, that we would be bringing her grain today," he said, halfway smiling and halfway disgusted.

"Hook that rope on her now. I'll take the bucket."

We led Haley Roo back towards the tack room, and towards the hitching post. She seemed as gentle as a baby lamb, walking with us, with her nose stretching a little now and then towards the grain bucket in Mr. Newman's hand. I felt a little better. Maybe things would go good now.

"Let's tie her to the hitching post and you can brush her," said Mr. Newman.

We tied her up with the quick-release knot that Mr. Newman had shown us when Roger first got Nevada Sage.

I went and got two brushes and a comb for her tail. When I walked up to her, she turned her head to look at me. She sure looks at me funny, I thought. I started brushing her with the curry brush, while Dad and Mr. Newman talked, and Roger came up to pat Haley Roo on her nose. She didn't seem to mind the brushing or Roger petting her. Roger walked around to stand by me and picked up the soft brush and stood ready to hand it to me.

Abruptly, instantaneously without warning, Haley Roo pulled back on her lead rope, made her eyeballs twice as big as what she was born with, and tried to detach herself from the hitching post. First her legs went out in different directions, then her hind end tucked under her bulging, heaving body. She pulled and pulled, then finally gave up and stood there looking at us as calmly as before she pulled. It scared me, and I think it even scared Dad and Roger too.

"Oh boy," said Dad. "This isn't a good thing."

Mr. Newman didn't say anything. Dad had already said it.

"Nevada never did this," said Roger.

"I think I'll have Buck and some of the boys come over to take a look at her," said Mr. Newman. "See if you can catch her tomorrow, first, just by walking up to her. Then try the grain again. Paul, if you want to, you could try swinging the rope again, or call me over to do it. If she keeps this stuff up, there's a way to make it easier for her to be caught. We might have to put a tire on the end of her lead rope. Wait until we get over here tomorrow to tie her. This exploding at the hitching post is something we have to be careful with."

"What's wrong with her, Mr. Newman?" I said.

"I think we may have a pretty spoiled mare here," he said. "Sometimes when a horse is used by kids and repeatedly gets away with things, it's harder for adults to deal with them when they expect things from them. You mix that with a smart brain, and a not so submissive personality, and you have a 1200-pound problem. But we'll see. Let's see how she rides tomorrow."

"I'll ride her!" said Roger.

"No you won't," said Dad. "I guess I could try riding her," he said to Mr. Newman. "I sure don't want Lissy on her yet."

"Let's have the boys come over and ride her tomorrow, Paul. She may mellow out and be okay."

Mr. Newman could see how bad I was feeling. "Don't worry Lissy. You'll get things worked out. You'll be riding with everybody else before too long."

"Thank you for helping us Mr. Newman." I said. "Should I... just put her back right now?"

"If you feel better doing that, why don't you," he said.

I brought Haley Roo out away from the hitching post, and let her loose. She trotted off away from me. The lack of répore between us was pitiful. I felt pitiful. I walked into the house dejected and feeling not just unloved, but totally unliked, by the horse that I thought would bring me so much happiness, and confidence around the other riders.

Gerdie never showed up that day - or the next one.

It was 'irresponsible' as the adults around me had called it. But it did give me time to find out about Haley Roo. Just what our future was to be together. Or if there even was one.

17

Cowboy Poetry

"I once had a mangy ol' horse.
Her trot an' her mouth they war' course.
Hit wrong on a bump, slid back to her rump,
An' was thrown to th' ground in remorse."

- S.J.L.

The next day came quickly. Since I didn't have happy anticipation, the day didn't drag on like most days did when you looked forward to something.

I got up. Fed the horses. Went to school, came home, and waited for Buck and the boys to come over. It was such good weather for doing things outside. Not too hot and not too cold. How strange that some days are so nice for such difficult circumstances. I should be thankful, I thought, and I was usually so glad when Buck was coming over, but today I sort of dreaded it. He would come over with 'the boys' and see how stupid I was. They all would. I had to swallow my pride and go through this thing. Couldn't they get here soon and get this over with?

I heard Buck's truck in Mr. Newman's driveway. I heard doors slamming, and voices. They went into Mr. Newman's house. I have to do something, I thought. I felt so stupid. I ran and got the lead rope to Haley Roo's halter and went into the tack room and got a little grain in a bucket. I set the bucket on the ground. I hooked the rope to Haley Roo's halter while she almost vacuumed up the grain. I grabbed onto her mane and swung myself up on her. She was harder to get on than Nevada was, since she was so much taller, but I made it. She stood chewing on the last bits of grain in her mouth while I sat there looking down at her broad withers and the top of her burnt red head. I pressed her sides. She started walking. We went halfway around the corral. She stopped suddenly and wouldn't move.

"Come on, let's go, Haley Roo!" I said quietly to her.

Mr. Newman and Buck and the boys were walking over to our yard. They saw me and stopped talking among themselves. Haley Roo started walking again. I pressed her sides to make her trot. She did, a little reluctantly, and we went around our riding area about halfway. The wind had come up a little. I didn't notice it too much, except that the tree leaves by our back lawn were rustling a little. Then she spied it. 'It' was a paper bag blowing through our pasture. She looked at it like it was a phantom, jumped sideways, and almost knocked me off of her back.

We walked along for a few more seconds, before

a small group of quail suddenly ran out from a bush outside of our fence. She jumped again sideways, as if those little birds with their tiny little babies were going to catch and eat her like a mountain lion. It was scary when she did that. My palms got sweaty and I felt a little sick.

"Hang on Lissy," said Buck. "She's just trying to get your goat."

I rode her towards Buck and everyone there and asked them, "Why does she do that? Is she scared? It's sort of nerve wracking."

"She knows that," said Moe, one of the young cowboys that worked on Buck's father's ranch. Moesell, with his blond hair and green eyes, and Dillard, dark and blue-eyed, who were in their early twenties, brown haired Pinky, almost seventeen, so tall and thin, who was Mr. Newman's great nephew from Genoa, and Toolie, one of the older cowboys, had all come over to see the "problem Appy" that the "Bloomingson girl" had "bought" from Gerdie.

"She's picking out booger men to spook at," said Dill.

"What do you mean?" I said. Haley Roo suddenly jumped again from who knows what, and this time she managed to dump me off of her barrel-round back with a buck. I hit the ground hard. It wasn't as bad as if I had been riding her fast, and was thrown high into the air, but it did stop my breath for a minute. It was as if the ground had flown up to hit me, because I was down on it so quickly.

"Are you okay?" they all asked at about the same time.

Buck and Pinky helped me up. My legs were shaking. I hoped that none of them would notice.

"Feel a little shaky?" said Moesell, smiling. He was enjoying every minute of my misery, I thought. I started to feel hot on the back of my neck inside my shirt.

"I'm okay!" I said. Here I was scared to death, and trying to ride this spooky horse, and he was getting a big kick out of it. Probably everybody was… I was angry.

"Well, don't feel too bad," said Moe. "We all get the spooks sometimes from spooky horses. You actually did pretty good up there kid."

"That's right," said Pinky. "She's just picking out things to spook at to give you a hard time."

From that time on I felt okay. I had a disappointing horse, a scary ride, and an embarrassing 'horse trade' to outlive, but I felt okay around Buck and the boys – not so much the oddball. That one sentence of encouragement from Moe, and the backup of Pinky and the other guys made all the difference. It's amazing what an ounce of encouragement can mean to a person in the middle of a desperate situation.

Mr. Newman had been standing there the whole time studying things. He was smiling now. "Let's see what the boys can do with this horse Lissy. It would be better for you to mind what your Dad said and stay off of her for now."

"I'll be happy to Mr. Newman." I was feeling guilty for disobeying Dad, and was so thankful that nothing worse had happened.

"Well why don't you guys put this horse on the hitchin' post an' jes see what she does t'day," said Toolie. He stood back with Mr. Newman to watch and study things. This was going to be interesting, I thought. Thank God I was feeling better.

Moe walked towards Haley Roo. He reached for her lead rope. Haley Roo, turned around, put her rump to him, and trotted quickly away. Moe instantly ran along side of her around to the front, and jumped on her around the neck, grabbed her rope, and led her back to us.

"Wow," I said.

Roger had got home and just come into the back yard. "Wow Lissy!" did you see that!"

"Pretty neat, huh Roger!" I said back to him quietly.

Moe and the rest of the cowboys just smiled, and went about their work methodically as if it was an everyday occurrence.

First they tied Haley Roo up to the hitching rail.

"Here Lissy," said Dill, handing me one of the horse brushes. "Walk up to her as if you're going to brush her. Just don't get under her feet or behind her."

I walked up to her slowly, trying to be as casual as I could, with my knees feeling a little jellowy. Her head was tied up close to the hitching rail. She couldn't turn it very far to see me, so she looked at me sideways, with her eye rolled back and beaded on my approaching body. I noticed her eyeballs even more today than ever before. The whites around the brown centers were actually red! She had red eyeballs! My palms began to get sweaty. Could she smell my fear? In more ways than one, Haley Roo could see me coming. She turned her head back towards the hitching rail and exploded. Feet everywhere, rump tucked under, head pulling back and forth, then S...NAAAPPP!! Her halter broke on her cheek somewhere. It had looked a little worn, but I didn't know how bad. She shot backwards toward the pasture. It's a good thing nobody was behind her. No wonder Dill had told me to not get under her feet.

Dad had just got home and came outside. "You have another halter for her don't you Lissy?" he said.

"I'll go get it," I told him. As I ran to the tack room, I remembered Gerdie handing me the other halter saying something like, "Here's her other halter, IN CASE YOU NEED IT." Almost as if Gerdie knew something like this would happen. Boy I'd like to tell that Gerdie a thing or two, I thought to myself...

"Hooaa...there girl! Easy up, there!" Dill and Moe were both running after Haley Roo, with Pinky walking after them with a rope in his hand. Haley Roo was running at top speed around our pasture.

Dad said to Roger, "Stay by the fence, son. Careful Lissy."

Haley Roo was a willful horse and seemed to think that she would outlast us all

I brought the new halter to Pinky, then I ran back towards the fence.

Mr. Newman, Dad and Toolie were all talking quietly in a group with Roger hanging on to their every word.

Pinky had lassoed Haley Roo. We could tell she didn't like it, but knew that she had been 'caught.' She walked back with Pinky leading her like a docile little 'puddy tat.'

"Boy, she's a real stinker, isn't she!" Roger said, while petting Nevada Sage through the pipe corral that he was temporarily locked up in. I looked at him, and he didn't say anymore.

The older cowboy, Toolie, said, "I've seen worse. Why don't you put 'er on thet post over thar."

The three younger cowboys brought her over to the post. Buck brought over a heavier lead rope and hooked it onto the spare halter - the one that read, 'Hâlé Roux' on it. Then Buck put the halter on her, and Pinky took off the rope from around her neck. They tied her to the tall, heavy post out in the right side of our pasture that had been part of the old fence that was up when we had moved in. As soon as she was tied, she exploded again. Cowboys scattered, and Mr. Newman, Dad, Toolie, Roger and I, all shook our heads.

"Mr. Newman," I said, "Why is she like this?"

"We don't know what she's been through in her past, and who owned her. I don't think she's scared. I think she's spoiled. Somebody must have let her get away with this type of stuff, or just maybe didn't know what to do about it. "

"Are Appaloosa's bad horses?" said Roger.

Mom came out into the backyard to see how things were going.

"Hi Katy," said Mr. Newman.

"Howdy Maam," said Toolie.

"Hello there," she said, smiling.

"They're not necessarily bad," said Mr. Newman. Some people have some great Appaloosas that they're very happy with. But I think they're smart and wiley. When you have problems with that kind of horse, it can be very difficult to deal with."

"There's a saying - up in the state of Oregon, I think," said Moe. "It goes something like, "Don't give me a bad time today, I've already had an Appaloosa morning."

Everybody laughed. We could all identify with that saying now, and laughing seemed to help a little.

"It's funny though," said Toolie, as I studied his scruffy profile and brown weathered cowboy hat at the top of his thin body, "there's old Hank Arrnsome and his Appy gelding, Marlowe. Why he jus' loves thet horse. I always said thet if Marlowe were a woman, and Peggy Ann, his wife warn't here, he would marry thet horse and be th' happier fer it…" Toolie caught himself up short, when he remembered Mom was out there. "Oh excuse me maam, beggin' yer pardon," he said to Mom, and sheepishly added, "It's just that Marlowe would *listen* to Hank, where Peggy Ann, nary a time, *would* not." He put his head down with a sorry look, and shook it with a little smile.

It would have been better if he hadn't added all that, because Mom looked embarrassed and just laughed a little, and I felt sort of funny too, but our thoughts were soon turned back to Haley Roo, because she hadn't stopped pulling at the post. In fact, she had gone in circles so many times around it, wrapping her lead rope around, until her muzzle was actually squished up so tight against the post, that her nose holes looked like they were shut too tight to breath through. It was truly a battle of the will. Haley Roo was a willful horse, and seemed to think that she would outlast us all.

"How long will she do that?" I said.

"Until she gets too tired," said Buck.

"That may be a while," said Dill.

"Let's try something," said Moe. He got a small flake of hay, and walked over towards her. She stopped pulling immediately and walked a little ways around the post to unwrap herself. Moe shook his head, and put the hay back.

"Dill said, "You got a bridle for her?"

"Here," said Buck. He had brought one from Mr. Newman's tack room.

Dill unhooked Haley Roo from the post and put the bridle on her. She seemed fine. He put Nevada's blanket and saddle on her. She seemed fine. He walked her out into the middle of the pasture, and got on. The groundwork hadn't gone well, but maybe just being her boss during the riding would work.

Dill walked Haley around the perimeter of the pasture. She seemed fine. Then he got her into a little trot. She seemed fine. He did some legwork, as if he were cutting cattle, and she turned and turned and turned again, then stopped on a dime. Dill started her into a lope. She's done some cutting," he said. "Maybe she wasn't too bad at it."

Suddenly she spooked. What was it? The wind was still blowing a little. Was it the tarp by our hayshed rustling a little? Was it the three starlings that suddenly flew from the tack room to the roof of our house? Whatever it was, she used it to full advantage, jumping sideways, and offsetting Dill, who had kept his feet out of the stirrups in case anything like this happened. She picked up her two front feet about a foot from the ground and reared. Dill stayed on. He trotted her forward quickly, until she bucked, then off he flew into the same sandy dirt that I did, making me feel even, a little more, like one of the "guys."

"Are you okay, Dill!" we all called.

He got up pretty quickly after putting his hand to his hair and rubbing his fingers through it. He had dirt on his face, and was rubbing his shoulder. "That dad…blamed…horse," he said, then seeing Mom and I standing there, he didn't say anything more until he came over to stand by Dad and Mr. Newman.

"Let me try 'er," said Moe.

"No, wait a minute," said Toolie. "No use you young fellers bein' put out of workin' commission. You got a lot of ranch work ta do in the next few weeks." Toolie was the foreman of Buck's father's L/M Ranch. "Let me work a little with 'er."

Toolie was boss and no one argued. And the funny thing is, that's just what Haley Roo needed - a boss that you couldn't argue with.

Toolie walked over to her with confidence. She didn't

move. He took her reins and walked her out into the middle of the pasture. He held the ends of the reins in his hand, and walked up to the side of her with his shoulder pointed towards her. She moved away from him. He moved into her again. She moved away from him. He moved into her. She moved away from him. He kept doing this repeatedly, until they were going around in sort of a circle, almost like they were dancing. It was always him moving towards her - never her towards him. Then he stood in front of her, still holding her reins. He walked toward her. She didn't move backward fast enough for him. He snapped the end of the reins on her chest. Huh…huh," he said gruffly but quietly to her. She moved back, and back, and back and still back again, until she was at the far corner of the pasture with him. He turned her around and did the same thing, just barely touching her chest, until they were back over near us. He got up on her, and kept his feet out of the stirrups for a minute, then put them in and rode her in a little gentle jog, sort of between a walk and a trot. He did this for quite a while, as we all stood there quietly watching the older cowboy at work. She didn't spook or buck. As Toolie rode by us, he said, "Now I'm a takin' it easy with her t'day. Thar's not a rider thet cain't be throwed. What she needs is a little time and work."

'I wonder how that girl, Gerdie rode her," said Roger, as we all stood there with Mr. Newman, admiring Toolie's expertise.

"Gerdie," said Moe, "is a horse broker. She and her Aunt have horses going through their place all the time. She may not have even done much with this horse - although she's probably tough enough to. Somebody probably had this horse for their kids for a while, then didn't know what to do with her when she pulled things on them, so they sold her. She could have been a ranch horse at first, but probably no one knows."

"It's sort of sad," I said, "what happens to horses sometimes. Maybe people are just too dumb with them sometimes. Like me."

"Don't feel too bad, Lissy," said Mr. Newman. "We all make mistakes. Just learn from them."

"Do you think I should try to work with her?" I asked. "Will she be okay?" Someone had walked up behind me while I was talking.

Toolie had ridden Haley Roo back over to us and got off. "She'll never be okay Lissy," he said. "Not fer you. She's been let go too long. She's unpredictable."

"She's also a mare," said Moe. "Sometimes girls are more difficult to deal with than a good gelding." He was smiling as he said that. I turned around, and who had come into our cozy cowboy group, but Pearl 'Peachy' Blayne.

"Oh, so little Lissy is having horse trouble?" she said, smiling back at Moe. "Howdy boys," she said.

"Howdy Pearl," the three younger cowboys all said to her. It almost sounded like a little song. Buck wasn't standing there with them. He was over taking the reins from Toolie and putting the halter back on Haley Roo for me.

"Let's tote this critter back over ta Gerdie's," said Toolie while he rubbed the top of Haley Roo's head. Haley Roo, to the surprise of all of us, pushed her nose with a little nudge on Toolie's arm.

"You like me rubbin' yer head, you crazy critter? You really like thet, don't you!" He rubbed her head some more, and she shut her eyes half way, and let her bottom lip sag a little. She seemed to actually like Toolie."

"I think she likes you, Mr. Toolie," said Roger.

"Well it might sound crazy, but I might jes try ta do somethin' with this here mare. We'll see. I'm a goin' ta give Gerdie what fer, fer heapin' this huge pile o' trouble on you though, Lissy. She should 'a been more careful."

"I think he's right," said Mr. Newman. "You need a different kind of horse, Lissy."

Pearl was over standing close to Moe and talking to him. It was almost as if she had singled him out today to bestow her uttermost attention on. Vexation crept up on me like a lion. Just those few words from her had set me on a bad track again. Buck glanced over there for a second towards them, and then glanced at me for a minute, but he was busy talking with Toolie about how he had dealt with Haley Roo today. What was he thinking when he looked at them, I wondered. Then Mr. Newman, Buck, Dad, and Roger were all in deep conversation with Toolie. I couldn't blame them.

It was pretty neat how he did things. His work with horses was like poetry. I just wasn't too thrilled about anything right now. I said very quietly to Dad, "Can I go into the house now?"

"Sure, he said. "Lissy, I'll talk to you when I come in, in a minute, okay?" he said quietly back. I could tell he knew how bad I felt, and that he felt bad for me too. I had caused so much trouble for it seemed like, almost the whole world.

Mom had gone into the house a few minutes before me, to start dinner. She didn't say anything when I came in. She just gave me a big hug, then went over towards the refrigerator to get out some lettuce. I didn't know what to do with myself, so I went to my room and waited, while Buck and Toolie and the boys loaded up Haley Roo into Mr. Newman's horse trailer and hauled her away with Buck's truck, back to Gerdie, the horse broker's, 'ranch.'

18

Sour Berries

It was Saturday. When I woke up that morning everything hit me like a bucket of cold water.

"Ohhh…" I moaned and flipped around in my bed
hoping to go back to sleep in peaceful oblivion. "Ohhh…"
I moaned again. It actually felt good to moan, and good
to feel sorry for myself. "Ohhh…oh…oh…oh…oh…" I
began making little songs with the word "oh" to tunes
like "There's No Place Like Home" and "Oh how I want
To Go Home" and "How Dry I Am."

Roger came into my room. "What are you doing
Lissy?" he asked with a smile that said "silly" on his
face.

"Nothing. Go away, Roger Muskrat Poopy," I said
to him, putting my head under the covers. Boy, did I
open up the floodgates for silly poopiness from Roger
that morning. I should have known.

"Hi Lissy Poopy-Doopy!" he yelled in ecstasy. "Lissy
Snoopy Droopy Goopy POOPIE!"

He sat on my bed.

"Get off my bed," I yelled!

"I'm not hurting your bed!"

"Yes you are, you're getting it all poopy!"

"I am not!"

"Where's Mom?"

"Out in the backyard with Dad and Mr. Newman."

"What are they doing?"

"They're talking about you."

"They are? How do you know?"

"Because I've been out there."

"In your pajamas?"

"Sure. I don't care about that. As long as it's warm enough, and I have underpants on, I don't…"

"What are they saying?"

"Oh, they're just talking about you and horses and stuff."

I pulled the covers off of my head and sat up.

"Like what stuff?" I said.

"Mr. Newman says that you're going through the "sour berries" portion of horse ownership. What does portion mean? Is that the same as the "food portion" on the mashed potatoes commercial on T.V.?"

I was deep in thought. "I think so," I said almost mechanically.

"Know what else they said?"

"What?"

"I'm not gonna tell you…!"

"Well go out then!" I threw my pillow at him.

"Lissy, how come you're so mad at me today!"

"I...don't know...I don't know," I said, while starting to sob quietly with my face in my covers.

Roger didn't say anything . After crying for a minute I looked up to see if he was still sitting on my bed. He was.

"Buck is there too," he finally said. "He's helping Mr. Newman move his new wood stove into the house. They're taking the old one out first, though. I'm going to ask them if I can have it!" Roger got up from my bed and jumped around in an excited little circle in the middle of the room, then left to put his play clothes on.

Buck is there too? I'd better get moving, I thought. I wanted to thank him and Mr. Newman for trying to help yesterday. I felt bad that I hadn't thanked the other cowboys. Maybe they understood.

I threw on my shirt and pants, but I couldn't find my hairbrush. "Where is it," I snarled quietly. I kept looking. I absolutely couldn't find it, or had no idea where it might be. Then I bumped my toe on the corner roller at the bottom of my bedpost. "Aaaauugghhhh!" I yelled. "Who cares, anyway!" I said loudly. "Who cares if I look like swamp woman and can never find my brush again, and never ever comb my stupid hair again!" Then I messed my hair up with my hands all over my head and fell back down on my bed and cried.

Mom looked into my room. "What's going on Lissy?" she said.

Roger was standing there looking into my room too.

I sat up in bed and he exploded into laughter.

What met their eyes was a very strange sight, both horrible and funny in a silly sort of way. I was sitting on the bed with my hair sticking out asunder. It was in every direction that hair could go, be it north, south, east or west, with my face hot and sweaty and my eyeballs wet and itchy under tightly clenched fists.

Roger was in a fit. He couldn't stop laughing. It was by far the most excellent sighting he had ever had of me.

"Oh Mom," he yelled. "Look at her! Look at her! Lissy you should see yourself! Look in the mirror! Your face is red almost like you have jelly on your cheeks, and your hair..."

"Roger!" said Mom. "You go out right now. I want to talk to Lissy. Out now!"

"Okay," he said. "But don't comb it down Lissy, until you look in the mirror!"

Mom turned to me, and the flying bush on my head, and I thought I saw a smile begin to sneak its way onto her face. "Lissy," she started quickly. "Lissy, I'm not going to say 'what's wrong' because I know what's wrong. You've had a real disappointing time lately. But your temper...I know about you throwing your clothes all over your room last night."

"You do?"

"Yes, I know a thing or two from time to time."

"Well it's just been so hard not to get mad. I 've been trying so hard to make things better. And it never works out."

"You've been trying in the wrong way," said Mom.

"I just started out trying to get a neat horse, and to not let Pearl Blayne always be 'the big winner.' Why is it so wrong to want to be as good as the other girls around here and their super-powered horses and their wonderful hair, and everybody thinks they're so great!"

"That's what I'm talking about," said Mom. "Trying to get a horse at the cost of throwing obedience and common sense out the window, to outdo Pearl Blayne, is the wrong way to do things. In fact, it has become a monster in your life. When you start operating like that you get worse and worse. Think moral. Keep your wits about you. We wanted so much for you to enjoy getting a horse. Dad and I didn't want it to be a horrible trauma and disappointment."

"I know," I said. "But what do I do? I'm a mess." I started crying again.

Mom smoothed down my hair, and she had that little smile on her face again while she looked at my head. Only this time she didn't hide it.

"The best thing you can do right now is ask God to help you overcome this problem. Ask him to help you with the steps to take. He can help you with obsessions and temper problems too. At first it will feel icky and annoying to do things the right way when you're upset or angry, but the more you chose the right way, the better it will feel." She hugged me. "I love you, messy or not! Come out and have some breakfast. Time to start a new day!"

"Okay," I said. "It's funny. I was just lecturing Roger on this sort of stuff not too long ago, and here I am being a moron myself." I stopped talking and looked around my room. "I sure would like to know where my hairbrush is."

Mom looked around the room too. "What's that?" she said. She was pointing to the top of my curtain rod that held my valance up over my window.

"My brush! I must have thrown it up there by accident last night when I threw my clothes around. I feel so stupid."

"Join the rest of the human race," she said, as she reached up and got my hairbrush for me, then threw it to me through the air.

I was finally ready, and made it outside. It was nice weather. I would have enjoyed it even more if I didn't remember the fact that too much nice weather in our snow months can lead to drought seasons with fires and dead trees, not so pretty sagebrush, and wild animals not having enough water in their regular areas of survival. I guess those responsible adults that I had thought were so silly and worrisome did know something after all. Why did I see it so clearly now. The other day in the cafeteria when I was on my 'high horse' I couldn't see a thing. Some people like me, I guess, just have to be practically hit over the head with a hammer …

I went out side to see Buck. I heard noises and voices in the front yard.

"Majesty can make it to the reservoir in record time and not even breath heavy!"

"Oh come on Pearl," said a familiar voice. It was Buck's.

"I bet he can outdo that cow horse of yours, Buck," she said back.

"He won't outdo Rooster, here," said another voice.

Oh no, it was Pearl and Riva out there with Buck again. Is there no end to the misery and unfairness of life? I walked around to the front of our houses. I had on my blue paisley shirt with blue Levis. Pearl was all gussied up in a red and black plaid shirt with black Levis and a small red silky scarf around her neck, with silver earrings that matched a filigreed silver bracelet on her wrist, and soft pink polish on her fingernails. Majesty had a fancy breast strap added to his black and silver saddle. The two of them looked like they were ready to be in a parade. Black haired Riva was her natural beautiful self, wearing just a touch of pink lipstick, sitting with one leg swung up over her saddle horn, on her handsome red horse, Rooster. Oh Lord, I thought, I don't have to be the cowboy queen of the continent, but could I not feel so darn bad about myself?

Pearl just ignored me. I must have been demoted to an even lower level on Pearl's list, because there wasn't even a, "Oh hi, little Lissy," or "Too bad about your horse, you little nincompoop," coming from her today.

"C'mon Buck, get Quick saddled up and let's go riding," she said in her babyish singsong, nagging voice.

*The two of them looked like they were
ready to be in a parade*

While she said that, she looked at him with eyes that were more like a thirty-year-old lover.

Okay, I'm leaving, I thought. I turned to go back around to our backyard, when Buck said, "Wait a minute, Lissy. I want to talk to you. I'll be right back." He went towards Mr. Newman's back yard.

I'll be right back? What, and you want me to stand here alone and talk to these two by myself? What are you thinking Buck? I stood there without saying anything, just looking down at Majesty's feet and comparing them to the size of Rooster's. They were about the same.

"So little Lissy is still without a horse." Well here it comes now, I thought. The dagger turns in Pearl Blayne's hand.

"Yes Pearl," I said, "I have experienced the sour berries of horse ownership." I surprised myself. I was tired of suffering over her ridiculous fol de rol. In fact, I didn't even care what she thought.

"Sour berries? Who thought that up? You? Well I guess that IS a cute way for a little girl to put it, for buying a horse that she can't handle…"

"Actually, that's my line," said a voice from behind us towards the house. It was Mr. Newman walking over.

"Oh…" said Pearl, in a timid way, and a little in shock.

"I've been through it, Toolie Weeks has been through it, there's hardly a horse owner worth his salt, who hasn't. We learn through the tough things and the mistakes that we make."

She sat there on Majesty in a silent limbo. With rational truth and common sense coming at her like a catapult, Pearl Blayne didn't have anything of worthwhile value to say.

Buck came around the corner leading Quick, who was all saddled up. He walked over to me and said, "Here Lissy, you take Quick for a ride with the girls. He needs some exercise, and I need to stay here and help Grandpa some more with his stovepipe connection. Got to go into the attic," he said with a smile, looking up at Pearl.

"Buck," I said quietly, "I can't keep up with them...I..."

"Yes you can Lissy." We were both on the other side of Quick from the girls. "Lissy, you're a good rider. I've watched you. You just need to be more confident. Quick's a good horse. You can depend on him. He isn't fancy looking but he's loyal. And he's FAST."

"He is?" I said. I could feel something start to pump through my veins, and it wasn't just blood.

Buck nodded his head, and smiled.

"Okay," I said, while Buck gave me a 'leg up' on Quick. I didn't really need a leg up, since I could get on okay myself, but I noticed that it was just sort of a nice gesture that riders would do for one another sometimes. "Tell Mom for me that I went riding, okay Buck?"

"Sure thing," he said, grinning.

I didn't even look at Pearl's face as we started off.

I knew she must be in a stewpot because Buck wasn't coming.

"Where are we headed for?" I asked Riva. Right now I figured she was the best one to talk to.

"To the reservoir," she said. "It's really neat out there." Riva was eighteen. She seemed a little older acting than Pearl. In place of the unabashed pettiness of Pearl, she was just pleasant and confident, and rode her horse Rooster, like a friendly Prom Queen.

"Let's go!" said Pearl suddenly. Off she sprang on Majesty, with Riva taking up her challenge like it was breathing. I guess she was used to Pearl doing that to her.

Quick kept his cool, but I could sense that he wanted to run too. He waited for me to tell him though. What a good horse! I thought. I leaned forward just the slightest bit, with my legs hugging a little closer to him. He was off like a bullet. Quick wasn't a whole lot taller than Nevada Sage, but boy could he run! He's a team roper, I remembered! We watched Buck do team roping at the fairgrounds. They would charge out into the arena as soon as the cow's chute was opened, faster than water from a busted dam, to get as close as they could, as fast as they could, to that little steer. If Pearls plans were to leave me behind eating their dust, I didn't think she would make it happen. Not with Quick under me.

The three of us were pretty darn near neck to neck down the dirt road that led out to the main street. I started pulling up Quick because we were headed towards pavement. Pearl and Riva just kept going. They crossed over the road with clinking, scratching noises coming from their horses' hooves. It looked like they would make it okay, until Riva's horse, Rooster, was almost completely over to the dirt, when one of his hooves slipped, and his leg went half-way down under him. He kept from falling and regained his bearing, and Riva managed to stay on him, but she was pretty shook up by the time I had caught up with them.

"Gosh, Peachy," she almost screamed. "We better take it easy until we get out to the dirt by the reservoir."

"I know," said Pearl, in a know it all way. "It seems like we just get going, and a stupid street comes along!"

We trotted our horses at a more moderate pace for quite a while. I silently thanked God for that happening. The two 'confident' girls would be a little more careful now, hopefully, and maybe I would be able to keep up with them through Quick's speed and agility, instead of hair-brained risk.

Finally, we reached the open sage and the long stretch of dirt that led up to the tree-lined reservoir. Without any warning, Pearl took off on Majesty towards our destination. Riva went after her, and I, not being trained for the gates at Santa Anita, had to get my bearings for a second, then started Quick off behind them. We rode along the smooth stretch of dirt at a faster pace than I had ever gone before. Quick's stride was so smooth from the speed that it was like riding a stationary barrel, with feet moving back and forth underneath, but making no bumps or even waves for the rider. We were flying.

We were near the destination. The thick muddy reservoir with its clumps of Poplars and Aspens became larger to our eyes, and I could see the outline of its shores clearly now, with bushes and sage and little mud bogs in between bodies of still water. But the thing that I really noticed by the time we got there was that Quick was up with the other horses! He had eaten nobody's dirt, and neither had I!

Pearl turned her head to look at Riva, and caught me out of the corner of her eye. She did a double take at me, and looked sort of surprised. I just looked back at her with a little Mona Lisa smile. Actually, I didn't know what else to do, even though I was feeling pretty good at the time.

"I'm going over to the other side," said Pearl. Good grief, she took off so fast again. She was still racing. Does this girl ever quit and relax a little?

Riva and I turned our horses in the direction Pearl was going. We were walking them, to see what the best path would be to get to the other side. There was some dry dirt that came in towards the bodies of water, and some mud. I noticed that Quick avoided certain spots, and when I turned him to follow Pearl, he balked and wouldn't go into some of the muddy areas. Rooster did the same thing to Riva, so she steered him away from those areas too. Majesty had the same regards towards those areas as the other two horses, but Pearl pulled out her little crop that she had attached to her black and silver saddle, and gave him a little snap on the rump. I guess she was going 'cross country' across the mud bog, so she could be first to the other side. Majesty didn't want to go, but Pearl's intimidation, and Majesty's obedient nature led them right into the middle of one of the patches of squishy wet dirt.

Pearl and Majesty went a few yards on, until Majesty gave a few little jerks, stopped completely, then sunk up to his belly in the foreboding, grayish brown gunk.

"Oh my God!" said Pearl as she sunk into the mud with Majesty.

"Pearl," we said to her, "Pearl, we're coming!" Riva and I rode as far as we could, then we got off of our horses and walked up to the edge of the bog. Pearl was in a panic and Riva and I were pretty near to that too. Oh God, what do we do, I prayed silently. Please help us! I felt alone. I wished that Pearl's "Oh my God" had sounded like a real prayer.

"Pearl, throw us your reins!" I said. "We'll try to lead him out."

"Get off of him, too," said Riva. "I'll help you out, just give me your hand."

It's almost as if Pearl had stopped thinking and we had to do it for her.

"How far will he sink!" she cried. "Is he still going down?"

"No," we said.

"He's stopped going down, at least for now, but he looks like he's stuck tight," I said.

Riva helped Pearl out of the mud. Poor Majesty, with his weight, couldn't budge himself.

"C'mon Majesty!" I said to him, pulling at his head with the reins.

"C'mon boy!" said Riva. "Wait a minute. I've got some horse cookies on my saddle. Let's try those!"

Riva brought the cookies over and waved them towards Majesty's nose. We could tell that he smelled them, by his nose holes flexing a little bit, but his eyes were starting to get that wild, scared look that horses get, when they're going beyond the point of anything but getting away from their fearful circumstances.

"I don't think he can get out!" said Riva quietly to me. "I don't think he can get out at all!"

Pearl started to wail. She sat down on the murky shore in her black Levis and red plaid shirt and red scarf. Her legs were already full of mud, from the thighs down. Majesty worked his legs a little but got nowhere. For Pearl, Queen of the Continent, and Majesty, her handsome consort, it was not a majestic moment for either one of them.

"What do we do?" said Riva.

What do we do? She's asking me? She's almost two years older than me and she's asking ME what to do? God, you're the wise one, we need your help. Please tell us what to do!

The other two horses started to Mosey off.

"Riva," I said, "will you get our horses before they leave us here?" I was busy thinking.

180

"Okay!" she said.

A picture of something that happened when we had first moved to Carson Valley came into my mind. We were in our second house here, across the valley. We were digging around some old fence posts that Dad wanted to take out, in a slushy, snow soaked part of the pasture, and I had stepped in a spot that was full of soft soil, mixed with horse manure, when my foot sunk into the ground halfway up to my calf. I pulled my foot out and lost my shoe. I had to dig my shoe out of the muck with my hands. I had been so annoyed at the time. It was so icky. Now why does something stupid like this have to happen, I had complained, that day. Something so unnecessary and for no good reason…

I waded into the mud by Majesty's chest. It was funny, he seemed to calm down a little when I came up to him. He wasn't alone! He was glad to have me with him in his time of difficulty. I talked to him and patted his neck. "I think I can get you out, Mr. Majesty." I patted him again. He looked at me, and I thought he was saying, "Okay, I'm game. Go to it." I wondered then, and I still wonder if horses actually know pretty much what you're saying to them, and what you're trying to do when you're helping them and even what you're thinking sometimes!

I began to dig around his chest. I dug and dug and pulled the mud away in huge clumps. I threw it behind us and to the side of us, anywhere, to get it away from Majesty's legs. He began pulling up on one leg. The suction was strong, but as I pulled out a little more mud each time, he would pull on his leg a little. Then he tried the other one. It looked like he was releasing his long limbs from the mud! He gave a little jerk, then a little lunge, and... "Ooommpphhh! ..." he gave a deep horse groan, and was crawling out of the mud in big jumps and lunges, as I stood to the side of him.

Riva began yelling, "He's out, he's out! Oh Lissy you got him out!"

I sat down in the middle of the mud bog. All of a sudden I was tired. I had mud all over me, but I hadn't really noticed until now. I even had to wipe some mud off of my upper lip with a little mudless patch of my shirt collar. "Does he look okay, Riva?" I called to her. "Can he walk okay?"

"I think so," she said. She led the other horses up to Majesty and grabbed his dragging reins. He was covered in mud too, except for his back and head. "Oh no, he's gonna shake now!" said Riva, still holding onto him. When he was done, she had small mud flecks all over her face and on her clothes. She just shrugged. She was as relieved as I was to get poor Majesty free.

Pearl had been crying the whole time. She went over to Majesty and hugged him around the neck and cried some more.

"He'll be okay, Peachy," said Riva. "Let's start walking him back towards home."

The three of us walked, leading our horses, away from the reservoir and its trees and water and mud-bogs. We went down the wide dirt stretch that led back towards the main streets to our houses. Two kids were out with their dogs, walking through the sagebrush and patches of dead Russian Thistle. The boys studied us, then started laughing. We were so tired and wanted to just get home, that we didn't care a whole lot then if we were laughed at or not. It had been more of an emotional tiredness that had overcome us, from the fear that Majesty could have hurt himself to the point of destruction.

Pearl hardly said a word on the way back. Riva talked a little. We decided to get on our horses and ride slowly, watching to see if Majesty had injured any muscles or tendons. We would probably know better tomorrow, how he was going to be for sure.

By the time we got to my house, Buck and Mr. Newman were done with their work, and they were sitting on our front porch with Dad. When they saw us, they didn't laugh, but they sure had funny looks on their faces. They knew that something must have happened. The three of them got up and walked towards us.

"Hi," I said.

"Are you girls okay?" asked Dad.

"We're okay," said Riva. "We must look a sight, though."

Roger came out the front door. He walked up to us and stared. He kept looking at us, then grinned. "You look sort of like the mummy women! Like in that movie on T.V. – 'Black Scarab of the Living and the Dead."

Riva and I and Dad and Buck and Mr. Newman laughed.

Pearl was quiet. Then she said, "Majesty got stuck in the mud at the reservoir. Lissy dug him out. I'm going to take him home now and get his saddle off of him." We all looked at the mud encrusted saddle and breast strap with its silver décor peaking out between gobs and flecks of light brown dirt. "Thanks Lissy. I'm so glad you thought to do that."

I was sort of in shock. She had actually thanked me in a really thankful way!

"Well," I said, "I prayed to know what to do."

"Your prayer must have been answered," she said. "I sure didn't know what to do, I was so scared. I guess it was sort of like the sour berries of horse ownership." She smiled a little, then started walking towards her house up the road, leading Majesty by his reins.

"I'll go with you, Peachy," said Riva. "Thanks for all your help Lissy."

"Bye, Riva," I said.

When the girls were gone, Buck and I could finally talk.

"Buck, thanks for letting me use Quick, today. He's a great horse. You said he isn't fancy, but I think he's wonderful."

"I thought you'd feel that way about him," said Buck. "He's got a heart of gold, and I bet they didn't leave you two behind today."

"Not at all," I said. Buck was such a good friend. I

was so grateful to him for all of his good-hearted help. I think I realized then, that I was actually starting to love him.

"Don't be too hard on Pearl," he said.

"What?" I said. Did I hear him right?

"Yeah," he said. "I know she can be a real pain in the wazoo, sometimes, but there are things about her that, well, make her the way she is. I mean, don't let her get your goat, just like that crazy Haley Roo did, but I figure the two of them have reasons why they're the way they are."

"O...Okay," I said. "Well I guess he's been sucked in by her charms after all, I thought. My Buck. My best friend that any girl could have. Life is so strange. So up and down, like a little boat in a sea of nauseas waves. By the time the sun went down in our valley that day, I was glad in my heart that God had helped me save an innocent horse from trouble, low about some of the people in my life, in fact, a little angry, and pretty dog-gone disoriented for a person who lives in a valley that you can see clearly in for miles.

19

Awakenings

Mom wasn't feeling good the next day, so we stayed home from church. She felt cold and ached all over, so Dad and I brought her some soup and crackers. She decided to rest a little and see if she could fight off this thing that was making her feel under the weather.

Roger had been in a bad mood all morning because yesterday, he had called Henreid's house to see if they had a corral or hitching post to tie Nevada to, for when he rode up there to play. Henreid told Roger that they had a hitching rail and a small corral, but weren't going to be home after all, because they were all going to Damon's baseball game. Roger was angry. "Why didn't they call me to tell me!" he had complained to Mom and I. So today, Dad was letting him go over to Deedee's with Nevada. Roger always had a good time playing with her, but today he was sort of crabby as he set out to go to her house.

I was a little disconcerted myself today, but not completely unglued. I couldn't find my Crystal heart necklace. I had been looking for it for the last two days. I had worn it to school during the week but couldn't even remember taking it off before I went to bed. One day I forgot, and took a shower with it on. It was like a blank. I was hoping to find it in our laundry basket or on my bedroom floor. I didn't feel so negative though, as I had been a few days ago about everything that had happened. My trip to the reservoir had renewed my faith in God, my self-confidence, and my spirits in general, but I was still so confused about Buck and his attitude about Pearl. I just couldn't understand it, or him or anyone!

I came outside to give Ford some water on the front porch, and walked over to watch Sniffy hanging in one of our small Russian Olive trees. He looked funny. He had started to slip, then caught himself and hung there looking at Ford with his eyes and nose all scrunched up.

Roger was so preoccupied about how "'boring and stupid his life had become" since he couldn't play with the Journoir kids, that he did things without paying attention this morning. When he said good-bye to Dad and had set his foot in the stirrup and started to hop up on Nevada, he ended up very suddenly on the hard, cold, ground.

"Are you okay Roger?" called Dad.

"I'm okay," he called. There were little sandy rocks stuck to the palms of his hands and he shook his fingers like they hurt a little. "I forgot to do up my cinch." He brushed his hands on his pants. "I'll fix it."

Dad watched Roger put the saddle back up on Nevada. Roger wrapped the strap through the big ring on the saddle three times, made a three-sided loop, then pulled it through. He stuck the leftover part back through a little bit before he put the stirrup down from off of the saddle horn. As he mounted up and took off down the road, Dad looked after him, like he was concerned about him. Maybe he was even praying for him. I thought that was a good idea, and was feeling pretty sympathetic towards him, until I heard him talking to Ernest Snow, then I decided that he should be hung by his toenails.

"Bye, Roger Muskrat," I yelled to him over a bush in our yard.

"Bye," he said without animation. Boy, he really must be in a 'poor me' mode, I thought. But who am I to throw stones, after looking back at the last week in my own life.

"Hi Roger!"

"Hi Ernie."

Ernest Snow, a small boy who lived on the acres right across the road from ours and went to our church, hung onto the top of a fence rail in his front pasture and smiled at Roger.

"You sure have a nice horse there." Ernie was only a year behind Roger in school, but was very small for his age, and a little shy. "Mind if I walk along beside you for a little ways?" He looked like he would have loved to ride along with Roger but didn't ask to.

"Not now," said Roger. "I'm on my way up the street here to a friend's house. In a few days I'm going to the Journoirs' House." He acted so important. He was so busy being important and grumpy that he didn't even notice whether Ernest Snow said anything back to him or not. He didn't even say anything when Ernie had started to walk back down the long driveway that went to his house. I found out from his sister later, who thought that Roger was "mean", that Ernie didn't eat hardly any lunch that day and had said to his parents that he had a stomach ache and that he had cried the whole time when he brushed his teeth afterwards, until his mother and father had asked him what was the matter.

I watched Roger's back and Nevada's tail move up and down, going up the street for a minute. A magpie glided past Roger to light on a fence next to the road. It was pulling meat from a field mouse held tightly under its claw. Being pretty birds, their stark black and white bodies were noticed all over the valley. They were scavengers, even of their own kind, and hunters of small rodents. All business, like cannibal waiters in tuxedos, carving and serving their kill with a flourish...I think Roger saw it too. He turned his head away from the magpie and its dead mouse. I felt chilly. The predicted warm spell had been short-lived. Winter weather had finally come again for a spell in our valley. The sky was overcast with a snow fog. It had snowed a little last night and would probably snow again tonight. Roger would probably be glad to get to Deedee's house.

I went over to JoAnna's house for about three hours that day. I needed some information from one of her reference books for a school report I was doing. We worked on our reports together. Dad had dropped me off, and JoAnna's mother gave me a ride home. When I got home, Mom was gone and Dad was in the backyard with a neighbor man that I didn't know very well.

"Where's Mom!" I yelled to Dad out the back window.

"She's with Pearl," he yelled back.

With Pearl? Mom's with Pearl? Mom's sick! And what in the world is Mom doing with Pearl!

"What in the world is Mom doing with Pearl!" I yelled out the door.

"She had some kind of emergency. Mom felt a little better, so she could go help her today."

Emergency! Mom going to help her with an 'emergency.' Boy, first Buck getting sucked into her little schemes, and now MY OWN MOTHER! I was absolutely horsewhip boondoggled at the sidewinding efforts of such a… a boondoggling Sidewinder like Pearl.

"Where's Buck and Mr. Newman?" I said, walking out the door towards Dad.

"I'm not sure." "I think Buck is with your Mom and Pearl, and I think Mr. Newman's been in Genoa since early this morning.

"Dad, what in the world are they doing with Pearl?"

190

"I don't know, Lissy, but she needed some help, and I did say, I'm not sure if Buck is with her or not. Maybe he's in Genoa with Mr. Newman. Can you hold this end up for me Vince?" They were working on the large fence gate for our back pasture. It was a two-man job. Dad didn't usually do work on Sunday, but the gate had been dragging so badly and became even worse when Nevada had pushed on it one day, trying to get to a bag of horse cookies that Roger had forgot to put away.

"Okay," I said. "I guess I'll go see if Buck is next door."

Buck wasn't at Mr. Newman's. I went back home when Mom pulled up in our car.

She smiled at me, but looked a little tired.

We went into the house together, and I began a small tirade.

"Mom! What were you doing? Where did you go with Pearl?" I sounded a little bossy, even to myself. "Sometimes I just hate..." I started to spew my hatred of Pearl all over my mother. She just stood there looking at me until I stopped talking.

"Pearl's Dad had a heart attack. I went to the hospital with her. She came over crying. Mr. Newman and Buck were gone, and she doesn't have any relatives close by here. Then I went to Mrs. Dibbs house to help her get a prescription at the drug store for her mother. They both have the flu and feel worse than I do."

"Ohhh," I said quietly, with something resembling guilt, sneaking up on me. "Is Pearl's father okay?"

"They think it was a moderate attack, and he's out of the danger zone, but they're going to do some kind of procedure to unblock some arteries around his heart. The doctors think he'll do well, but Pearl was just beside herself with fear."

"Is she at the hospital now?"

"She'll be there for a while today. Her Aunt from Verdi came to be with her. I think she'll be okay."

"Poor Pearl," I said. How my thinking and demeanor had changed, within just a few seconds.

"Lissy, I had a little talk with Pearl. And she gave me this." Mom handed me my Crystal heart necklace.

"My necklace! How did she get it? Why would she have it?"

"You dropped it at the reservoir when you were there with the girls. The ring on the clasp is opened up a little, and as far as we can tell, it must have fallen off of your neck before you went into the mud with Pearl's horse. She saw it on the ground and put it in her pocket."

"And she gave it to you today?"

"Yes. She said that at first she wanted to keep it. But after you got Majesty out, her conscience wouldn't let her. She actually forgot about it when you three came home from the reservoir."

"She put it in her pocket when she was so upset about Majesty? Why would she bother at a time like that? And she has jewelry coming out her ears. Beautiful, expensive, jewelry!"

"I think she did that, because she has something else

that she's been upset about for a long time."

"She has? What in the world would that be?" Other than the heart attack problem, I couldn't see why Pearl would squawk about anything in her life. She seemed to have it made.

"I asked her if she wanted to call her mother from our house to tell her about her Dad," said Mom. "She said she didn't want to and told me that her mother had left her and her father when she was ten years old, for another man. She went to live with him in Louisiana. Pearl and her father haven't seen her since then."

"But what does that have to do with my necklace and stuff?"

"Pearl said that to her, it just seems like you have everything. You have a mother and father, and a good home life. People LIKE you - Buck and Mr. Newman, and the kids and neighbors around here. They just sort of put up with Pearl. Mr. Newman has helped her and her Dad for years, even though he gets annoyed at Pearl like we do. She's had a real struggle with jealousy and depression for a long time. It's hard for her to accept that her mother would leave her like that. She said it came as such a shock because her mother used to be affectionate to her and dress her up in pretty dresses and buy her things, and for some reason, she always called her "Peachy" instead of Pearl."

I sat down on a dining room chair. I think I actually felt a little dizzy. Part of the mystery of Pearl the Plunderer was now unfolding under my very nose. No wonder Buck had said the things that he did to me yesterday. He must have known these things about her, or at least some of them. He must think I'm a terrible, hateful person. I didn't want to be that way. It's just that Pearl had been so miserable to deal with.

"I guess this explains some things about her," I said to Mom.

"Yes," she said. "It's not an excuse for her behavior, but it is an explanation. I know plenty of people who have had terrible things happen to them, like your Dad in the Korean War, and they don't treat people terrible. In fact your Dad treats people wonderful even though he has a hard emotional time about the past. But you see, he has God helping him to treat people with love and not hatefulness. A lot of people don't have that. They're trying to live life on their own steam."

"Like Pearl!" I said. "But what do you do with a person like Pearl? Do you just let her steamroller over you because you feel sorry for her?"

"No, you stand up to her. But you don't hate her. It won't help her to enable her to pound on you and other people, but it won't help her to be hated. I think she may be growing up a little. Her Dad's going to need her help now. She said he's spoiled her for years with horses and clothes and just about anything she's wanted, because she's been hurting so bad, and he has plenty of money to do that. But she said that now she wants to help him because she loves him and he's been a good father in many ways, even though he's been somewhat

194

over indulgent. I gave her one of the New Testaments that we had in the car. I think she's going to read it."

"Wow, that's pretty wonderful," I said. It's a good thing, I thought, that God is more loving than me, and less concerned with all the stuff that human beings put so much importance on...if He wasn't, all of us humans would be in a real pickle.

I felt better after talking to Mom about Pearl, but I still felt uncomfortable and confused about other things. God understands me and forgives me, and I'm thankful for that, but what about Buck? What does HE really think of me?

20

The Rat Cheese

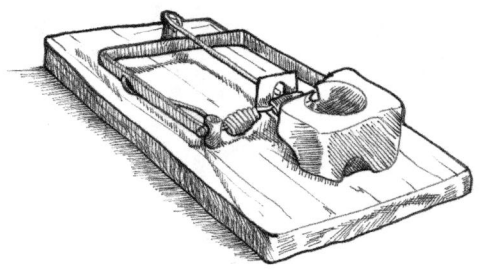

While I had been grappling with my problems of human psychology and the spiritual darkness of human folly in love matters, Roger had set out on his own journey of terror, and had been involved in a more physically dangerous spiritual battle. It was a pretty big one for a little guy of nine years old, to deal with.

I will tell you the story the best I can from what Roger told me about his day at the Journoirs' house. Yes, the Journoirs' house. While I was at JoAnna's, and Dad was busy with the fence, and Mom was with Pearl, Roger had gone to Deedee's house to play for a while.

Then her mother told her that she had to stop playing and go to town with her. Roger had been pretty disgruntled with that since he was already in a bad mood, and started to come home, but then he had turned around and decided to just mosey himself on up to the Journoirs' house, without asking anybody about it and no matter who cared where he went.

Roger had seen Ernie on our street again, and had told him he was heading up to the Journoir's house. Roger didn't have to elaborate to me, but I can imagine it was in pretty much the same snotty demeanor that he had used earlier when I had overheard him. Henreid had been playing in the street near his own house, when Roger saw him. Roger said he was glad to be leaving his house and going someplace else. Especially to a place where there were mostly older boys like him. Boys that could do a good job of taking care of themselves.

"Boy we're going to have fun today!" Henreid had said to Roger, and seemed openly hospitable to him. "And you brought your horse! Could I ride up there behind you?"

"Sure! C'mon up!"

Damon ran on ahead having no interest in horses, just like his older brother Derek.

"He's in a hurry to get back home," said Henreid. "We're working on the pipes again today. We want to get them all set up before it snows."

"The pipes?" said Roger. "Do you guys know how to fix the pipes in your house?"

"Not the pipes IN the house," said Henreid. "The ones ON the house. Derek says we're making a 'Rube Goldberg Extraordinaire'."

"What in the world is that?" asked Roger.

"It's a contraption, and you have to see it to believe it!"

The boys had come to the back corral fence of the Journoir's place. Their house faced the opposite way towards the next road over. The other three boys were in the backyard.

"Hi Roger!" called Babs. He was two years younger than Roger and Henreid but seemed just as old and involved in everything that the older boys did.

"Lift up the other end when I tell you to," Derek said to Damon. "Okay, NOW!" The two boys were holding a long gutter pipe, disconnected at both ends with right angle pieces. The pipes had been unhinged from the house, but now the two older boys were ready to attach them back to the house on a slant. There were all kinds of pipes coming from every which way around the sides of the house and one side had already been connected to a few white plastic rods leading up towards the peak of the roof. Roger said he had never seen so many different kinds of pipes before. It was a frightfully odd sight as his eyes traveled over the strange assortments of metal and plastic tubing. "Lissy," Roger had said to me later, "I felt like if I got shrunk down to the size of a mouse, I'd be lost like a rat in a maze and maybe never find my way out again!"

198

"We're going to put a steely into the pipes when they're all hooked together and see how far it goes!" Hendreid told Roger.

"Did...did you take off the drainpipes that your dad already had on the house and...move them?" asked Roger, directing his question more to Derek and Damon than to the younger boys.

Derek ignored Roger completely. Roger noticed that he was a serious, almost sad looking boy, who was usually only contented looking when he was making something mechanical. He was very good at making things, and many times, they really worked. His abilities were advanced for his age. Damon, who admired him greatly, called him a seventh grade genius, and tried, when he could, to imitate him, which sometimes worked but more often didn't.

"Oh, our Dad doesn't care..." said Damon.

"He doesn't KNOW," added Henreid.

"And Mom never comes out of the house in the back here," Damon continued.

"She only comes out of the house to go to town," said Babs factually. Babs always seemed to talk like a little old man, by the way Roger described him. A little old man, that he said sounded like he didn't like things the way they were, but was willing to face the truth.

"Let's go inside the house and play with my ouija board," said Damon to Roger.

"Okay. You have a weejie board?" Roger asked.

"Yeah. I got it for Christmas."

"Boy are you lucky. My mom and Dad won't let me have one."

"Why not?" asked Henreid as they walked into the house.

"Oh, they say that it's 'accult.' That it's not good to play with them."

"Oh yeah?" said Henreid with polite interest.

"Sometimes I think they're right," said Roger. "But it sure takes away my fun."

Henreid wasn't really paying attention now. He was busy pulling down a large cardboard box from a shelf in the closet of the boys' toy room.

The Journoir's house was large. The two older boys each had their own rooms. Henreid and Babs shared a bedroom, but there were two extra bedrooms in the house beside all of theirs, and Mr. and Mrs. Journoirs' spacious master bedroom. The house, Roger said, looked like rich people lived there. The furniture and things in it reminded him of our Great Aunt Tessie's house in San Francisco. He thought he had better remember to not sit on the furniture in his jeans, he said, especially if he got dirty playing outside. Then he saw Babs bring in a bowl of red jello, and eat it on the couch, spilling it, and wiping a few wiggly pieces off of it with his shirtsleeve.

The two boys played with the ouija board, asking questions about their future, and what the spirits behind the ouija board could tell them about dead people, and asked them to help them with having more 'power' over people. That was Henreid's idea, according to Roger.

Mrs. Journoir had come into the playroom once to say hello to Roger. She asked him if he liked tuna. They were having sandwiches and soup for lunch. Henreid had insisted on having grilled cheese sandwiches for lunch instead of tuna. Even after his mother had explained to him that she had already opened the tuna and wasn't sure if she had enough cheese...he had pounded his sacred wooden bird statue from the Fiji Islands, that he had been showing to Roger, very firmly on the floor, and said, "I don't want tuna, I want CHEESE!"

"Well, all right then," his mother had said. "Roger, I...I hope you like cheese too..."

"Uh, yes. Yes, I do, Mrs. Journoir. I like it fine," he had told her.

When it was time to eat those grilled cheese sandwiches, the boys all gathered in the large eating area off of the kitchen. Mrs. Journoir had set a nice lunch of sandwiches, soup, chips, stuffed celery, and hot chocolate out on the table. Then she retreated to her sitting room off of her flower-wallpapered bedroom with the matching curtains and furniture. She was drinking tea, Roger said, and looked very sad.

As the boys ate lunch, Roger listened to them talk. Listening, he thought, might tell him how to be able to say something to Derek, and have him answer back.

"Yeah, that was really pretty funny," said Derek shaking his head up and down, then sticking a potato chip in his mouth, letting it melt on his tongue. "We sure had old man Stephens running around like one of his chickens after he went 'whack!' to it." He swung his hand sideways towards Damon's neck.

"You let all of the chickens out?" asked Roger. "Did he catch them?"

Damon answered. "He caught them, but it sure was hard! Boy did he look funny running around." He leaned close to Roger and said quietly, "Don't tell anybody, but yesterday we let his big ole steer out into his neighbor's pasture. We watched from behind the sagebrush along the road. He was so mad!"

"We're going to have to be careful," said Derek, slowly stirring his soup. "I think he's getting wise to what's going on."

The front door opened.

"Dad! It must be Dad!" said Babs. He left the table and ran towards the living room.

Roger and Henreid were done eating, since they had done most of the listening and less of the talking. They went into the living room and watched T.V. for over an hour. Mrs. Journoir was talking to Mr. Journoir as they came into the living room. "I wish you didn't have to leave again."

"Sorry dear, I have to. The director's meeting is in Dallas this time. They scheduled it for tomorrow. I've got to go."

"Oh," she said.

He went to pack his suitcase and the boys played in the living room until he came out again. Henreid, Babs, and Damon were running through the house. Roger ran a little, then remembered that it was a big "NO" at his house. He wondered if it was here, too.

"Boys!" Mrs. Journoir said. "Stop running! I don't want to get bumped into again!" As she rubbed her arm, pushing her sweater sleeve up, Roger noticed a large black bruise running from her elbow up her arm on the inside.

The boys didn't stop running, and began pushing each other. Mrs. Journoir told them to stop, but they didn't seem to listen. Roger was bracing himself for a real waterloo. Mr. Journoir came into the room, again. Surely he would bring down fire and brimstone on at least Henreid and Damon - they were being so rough! But to Roger's amazement, all he said was, "Boys, boys," then laughed in a little, polite, "Ha ha… Ha ha… Ha ha ha."

"Well, dear, I won't be gone too long. Day after tomorrow I'll be back. See you later boys. Goodbye Roger."

The boys ignored him. They had run down the hallway into the playroom.

"Goodbye Mr. Journoir," said Roger. But Mr. Journoir didn't hear him because he had gone out to the front porch to say goodbye to Mrs. Journoir. She was sad looking again. Roger could see her through the front window with her hand on Mr. Journoir's arm.

"Roger!" Henreid called from down the hall. "Come here!"

Roger started towards the bedrooms.

"Over here!" said Henreid. He and Damon and Babs were in the laundry room. "C'mon."

Roger followed the boys past the washer and dryer and folding table, then out the door into a large room that had been built onto the main house for storage.

"Watch Damon," said Henreid. "He found the trap FIRST today."

"Watch him swipe the cheese!" said Babs.

They all looked down at the floor in a corner by the washtub. There was a hole about the size of an orange in the wooden floor. Right next to it was a rodent trap. A large one. Large enough to snap and kill a good size rat.

Damon held a plastic toy arrow in his hand. He seemed to be pointing at the trap. "S...NAAAPPP!"

What a loud terrible noise, thought Roger. "What is he doing?" he said.

"He's stealing the cheese," said Henreid. "Get it? He snaps the trap with the arrow, then takes the cheese."

Roger looked at the trap again. There was something reddish-brown on the flat wooden part. Blood! It was blood from a rat or mouse, he realized. "Isn't it kind of dirty to touch?" he said, looking at the icky piece of wood and wire.

"Ah, no big deal," said Damon. "We caught some mice with it in the garage a few weeks ago, but no rat yet."

"We steal the cheese," said Babs, "so Mom will think

that a rat keeps taking it. She's terrible 'fraid of rats," he said, talking like a little old man again.

"Yeah! It's a game," said Henreid. "Mom and Dad have been trying to catch that rat for a long time. But we play a game behind their back. Whoever sees the cheese in it first when they're not looking, steals it. Derek taught it to us," he added.

Roger looked at Damon. Damon looked at Roger. Then, as Roger could hardly believe what he was seeing, Damon popped the filthy cheese into his mouth and with two chews and one gulp it was gone.

"Damon..." said Roger. "Damon..." Roger said it was like talking to a person who had just swallowed a poison pill, but had no concern at all over it. If nothing worse, a person could very well get the barf flu from such germ-laden cheese, which is bad enough, Roger and I had both agreed.

"Ha ha ha," Damon laughed. So did Henreid and Babs.

"C'mere," said Damon. "I want to show you something else." He moved two boxes out of the way and looked down. "See?" he said. "Isn't that a stash!"

Roger looked into an opened box that Damon pointed to. Inside of it were smaller cases of candy bars. Candy bars with peanuts, candy bars with nougat, candy bars with coconut... chocolate, delicious, and...eaten! Half of the box had been hollowed out of candy, with the wrappers thrown back in.

"They don't know that we eat them," said Henreid in

almost a whisper. "Our Dad works for a candy company. He's a salesman and these are his samples. He flies all over the country. He gets so many cases, that he doesn't even know!"

"Don't you guys ever get sick?" asked Roger.

"Not usually," said Henreid. "Oh, once Babs threw up, but he's allergic to coconut."

Roger felt a little funny by then. He told me, that's when he had decided that he wanted to go home.

"What time is it?" he had asked Damon.

"Let's go to the kitchen and see," said Henreid. "We have a long time to play yet, I think."

The boys headed for the main house. They could hear Derek talking loudly to his mother in the kitchen. "I want you to move the wood TODAY, Derek," his mother said.

"But DAD didn't say I have too!" he almost yelled.

"Well, he was in a hurry with packing...."

"He's always in a hurry," he interrupted rudely. "If you want it moved today, do it yourself!" He went out into the backyard and slammed the door.

Roger could see by Mrs. Journoir's face, that she was very upset. The other boys didn't seem to notice.

"Henreid and Damon, go play in the toy room now," she said. She seemed to want to be by herself.

Hendreid, Damon, and Babs, all ran through the living room, down the hallway, and into the toy room. Roger didn't move. He stood in a corner in the kitchen. Mrs. Journoir was quietly crying. Roger said that while he was looking at Mrs. Journoir, he had almost the same feeling that he did once, for a cat that had been hit by a car and was laying at the side of the road meowing, but couldn't get up because it couldn't move its hind legs.

"Are...are you okay Mrs. Journoir?" he asked her very quietly.

"Yes...yes," she said, holding a kleenex up to her nose and eyes with her head tilted down.

"Maybe...maybe you could come to church one Sunday," he said. "My Mom would like to see you. She said that." Roger said he was trying to act normal but had stopped for a minute to swallow because he was so nervous and his mouth was very dry. "She said that she likes to visit with you."

"Well, maybe I can come -sniff- one Sunday -sniff- Roger." She looked at him with red, damp eyes. " Maybe I WILL come." She smiled at him. " You go play now, okay?"

"Okay," he said, and walked out of the kitchen.

Roger and I found out that even though Mrs. Journoir had been a Christian since she was a teenager, she hadn't paid attention to how God really wanted her to live for a long time. She had asked Him for help that very day right before Roger had invited her to church. Mrs. Journoir did come to church one month later. It was to be the turning point in her life and the life of her family. God provided just the sermon that she needed to hear. She would be reminded about the importance of honoring God in their lives, and to stay away from having anything occult, or other creepy things that were spiritually unhealthy in her house. She heard a sermon on "Discipline in the Home, According to the Bible" from which our parents got an earful at church too, and would be reminded of God's rules on discipline for the family. She would talk to her husband, who ended up coming to church a few months after she did, about what she had learned. He was very receptive and in turn, would put a stop to the disrespect and unhealthy activities of the boys, and turn their house into the home that it was meant to be. He would guide his boys at home, while God guided them through the hard, disciplining knocks of life in the outside world. They were tough nuts to crack, but not too tough for God to deal with. Derek especially, still got into some trouble off and on, but it wasn't as bad as it could have been. Mom had found these things out from Mrs. Journoir, when she would see her and talk to her at church. One good thing about Mrs. Journoir, she was no phony, and told it like it was, with a thankful heart towards God, who had helped her family so much. If Roger had known about this on that day he was over there, he wouldn't have been feeling as awful as he was. But I told him that usually when we're going through icky stuff, we just have to have faith in God for the outcome of difficult and scary things.

When Roger came into the playroom, only Henreid and Babs were there. After they had played for a while, Roger asked, "Where's Damon?" still having the urge to go home.

"He's outside," said Babs. He looked up at Roger, but then turned his head to the side with his mouth twisted up into a little grin.

Roger said that the way that Babs was acting made him feel a little funny, so he went over to look out of the window. The post that he had tied Nevada Sage to was in plain sight. But there was no Nevada.

"My horse!" he said. "He's gone!"

Babs giggled, then put his hand over his mouth. He looked at Roger.

"Why are you laughing? What's going on!" said Roger, with a little feel of panic crawling up the sides of his neck.

"Damon," Babs giggled again, "untied your horse to play a trick on you."

"Oh yeah," said Henreid, who was busy stuffing pieces of candy bar into his mouth while setting up strategic plans with little WWII soldiers on top of his ouija board. "Ha ha. He did say that he was going to do that. Ha ha."

Roger ran from the room, and from the house. It didn't matter anymore about the no running law. That was it. That was the last straw.

He looked in the backyard and spotted Damon.

"You...you...!" He said he was so angry that he couldn't even think of the bad names that he wasn't supposed to call anybody. He was afraid that Nevada had run away with the reins and halter rope dragging. If

Nevada spooked and ran he could trip and hurt himself pretty bad. He didn't bother to even ask Damon if that was the case, but went out to the road. Far down, he could see a horse trotting toward the west, towards our house, then turn off onto a side street. He was pretty sure it was Nevada.

Suddenly, from behind some large Sage bushes, Derek and Damon jumped out, and grabbed him.

"Hey, quit kicking, little squirt," said Derek.

"Let go of me!" Roger yelled at them.

"You know," Derek teased, "you're such a fun little guy, that, OW! Hey, I said quit kicking! Cut it out!" He lifted Roger up and had him by the shoulders, with his feet in the air almost over Damon's head.

Roger was in such a panic by then that he said he couldn't think straight, and just wanted to do anything to get away.

"Aw, let's let him go, Derek," said Damon. "He's just a little twirp." Then he laughed.

"No," said Derek. "I don't let little cowboy '- - - - kickers' go, who like to kick ME!"

"Then what do you want to do with him?" said Damon a little nervously.

"You'll see. Take his legs, and I'll take his HEAD." He looked into Roger's eyes with a threatening glare. Roger said he began praying then. He just asked God to help him.

The two older boys carried Roger up over a rise on the east side of the Journoirs' property. They had ten acres that butted up close to the BLM land in the first hilly area of the Pine Nut Mountains. They brought Roger to a little dilapidated shack of a house. Roger said that if the house had been a person, it would have looked like a "mummy ghost" to him. The house had been built in the 1890's. The part of the house above ground was completely rotted out with no floor left. The only substantial part of it was a root cellar, with a broken ladder going down into it. Derek hung Roger down into the cellar by his hands, and dropped him in. He and Damon pulled up the ladder.

Roger said he just stood there like a rabbit in a feed store cage. He didn't yell or say anything to them. He felt like they just weren't worth talking to. He told me he asked God to help him again. He sat down on the cement. He said he was in too much shock to cry. He couldn't believe anyone could be so mean. But he said that Ernest Snow came to mind as he sat there. He didn't know why. Ernest Snow – his face.

It was empty of anything but old broken boards and a few tin cans that were probably collector's items. There were spiders, which had never scared him, and a scorpion that ran across the floor of the cellar. He was careful where he sat, after seeing the scorpion. He didn't want a sting in addition to being imprisoned. The walls of the cellar were also slick cement, and Roger said he was pondering on how to get out of there. It wasn't terribly high, but there was just nothing at all to grab onto. Water started coming out of a hole towards the bottom

He was careful where he sat after seeing the scorpion

of one wall. Oh no, he had thought. Water! He said he prayed real hard that God would stop the water from coming in, and that it did stop!

It was getting late by the time that Roger had been bushwhacked and put into the cellar. Dad had called

Deedee's house and a few other places to try to track him down. He put his jacket on to go look for Roger in the car. Buck and Mr. Newman were back home. Mom was sort of worried now about Roger. She was mainly concerned that he had had a problem with Nevada and went too far from home chasing him or something.

I ran over towards Buck's house, but before I got there, I looked up the street. There was Nevada trotting down the road towards our house, with his reins dragging. He stopped for a minute to grab a bite of the weeds that were in the ditch at the east edge of Ernest Snow's property, then pulled his head up, and trotted across the street. I ran to get him. I started to feel scared for Roger. I brought Nevada to our front yard, then I went over to Mr. Newman's and I yelled to Buck.

"Buck! Buck!" It was only a few seconds before he came running out of the house.

"Did you find Roger?" he asked. Dad had already called Mr. Newman's house.

"No, and I just found Nevada coming down the street by himself! I'm worried about Roger!"

"Don't worry," said Buck. "My horses have come home without me a few times. And I'm still here!"

"Will you help me look for him? Dad's taking the car. I'm going on Nevada."

"Sure!" he said. "I'll go get Quick."

Pearl drove by the front of our house. She could tell something was wrong.

"What's the matter?" she yelled out of her car window.

"We're trying to find Roger," I said. "Have you seen him?"

"I saw him talking to Ernie Snow today," she said.

"Real early this morning?" I asked.

"No, not real early. It was more like eleven to eleven-thirty. My Aunt drove me home for a minute to get some things to bring to Dad at the hospital, then we went right back up there. Roger was on his horse when I saw him."

"Eleven to eleven-thirty? I wonder where he went then?"

"I'm going over to Riva's for a few minutes," she said, "and then I'll drive around to see if I can see him."

"Okay," I said. "Thanks Peachy! I hope your Dad gets well real soon!"

She looked a little surprised, then smiled at me while she rolled up her car window.

Buck was there with Quick, and Dad was getting into the car. I told them that Roger talked to Ernie again late this morning. Dad drove over to Ernie's. We hadn't gone to Ernie's before this or called his house because Roger never wanted to play with him and had been so stinky to him lately. Ernie told Dad that Roger had said he was going to the Journoirs' house today.

When Dad came back and told Buck and I about Roger, we all headed up to the house that my nervy little brother just HAD to visit that day.

"Boy, I would hate to be in Roger's cowboy boots tonight," I said to Buck as we trotted up the road. He's been so horribly mean to Ernie lately. Then he goes up to the Journoir's house like this. I'm surprised he would have the nerve…"

"Oh I'm not," said Buck. "I've got myself in a hot kettle of trouble before. He's not the first kid that ever went someplace he wasn't supposed to, or has done something dumb."

"Yeah, I know what you mean," I said, feeling embarrassed about myself, this last week.

Buck just laughed. Now what did that mean? Was I stupid looking to him? I had to concentrate on Roger. He was probably okay, being up at the Journoirs' - but what about Nevada running loose?

When we got up there, Dad was out of the car, coming back around from the front of the Journoirs' house. "Nobody's home," he said. He looked concerned.

"What do we do, Dad?" I didn't want to start crying like a fool, but I just felt so spooked about things, and the day was so gloomy…

Buck bent down on the ground and picked something up. It was the broken top half of a medium sized carrot. It looked like it hadn't been on the ground for too long.

"A carrot!" I said. "Roger carries a carrot in his pocket for Nevada a lot of times when he goes places and gives him pieces during his ride! Do you think he's somewhere around here, Dad?"

"Let's get looking!" said Buck. I could tell that he was finally a little nervous and concerned too. Why do boys take so much longer than girls to see the red light and hear the buzzer? Or do they just hide how they feel more?

We scattered on our horses towards the far north acreage, and Dad walked up over the rise of the east property. He saw the old house and headed towards it. "Hey, what's this over here!" he called to us, and waved us back. We got there before he did, and when we stopped we could hear a little voice singing from down inside the shell of the ghostly shack.

"Froggy went a courtin' and he did ride uh huh... Froggy went a courtin' and he did ride oh ohh... Froggy went a courtin' and he did ride, a sword and pistol by his side, uh huh ..."

"Roger! Is that you?" I yelled.

"Lissy! Lissy! It's me!"

Buck and I got off of our horses and went to the edge of the hole, through a broken wall of the house. Dad had run up to the broken wall too, and we all told Roger, not to worry, that we would get him out of there right away.

Roger started to cry, but kept singing "Froggy Went a Courtin" quietly, while he flexed his hands together in and out, like he couldn't hardly stand to wait any longer.

When Buck saw him start to cry, he said, "I figured it must be you Roger, because nobody else sings that awful!"

Roger gave him a big smile through his tears, while

Dad lowered the broken ladder into the cellar.

"Want me to go down in there Mr. Bloomingson?"

"I'd appreciate it Buck. You're a lot lighter than me. I don't know if that ladder will even hold you up, let alone me. Besides you heal quicker than I do." Men. They always seem to do those rough types of jokes when they're under stress, I thought. Not like girls who are more sensible, and just cry and hug.

Buck climbed down into the cellar and got Roger going up the ladder in front of him, and made sure that Roger wouldn't fall backward. Dad grabbed onto Roger and lifted him onto the dirt where I was standing. Then as Buck was coming up, the broken ladder crunched under the weight of his boot. Two of the rungs fell to the ground. Dad gave Buck a hand out, then Dad and I both hugged Roger while he stood there shaking, trying to tell us the whole story of the day, in about two frantic run-on sentences.

"Let's get into the car and go home, Roger," said Dad. You're awful cold. You can tell us everything that happened at home."

Buck and I rode the horses home. We were quiet. We were both relieved that Roger was safe now. It had shaken us up pretty good. Roger hurt his foot when he had been dropped into the cellar, and if we hadn't found him that evening with the temperatures going so low after dark, he could have froze to death. Dad would let Mr. and Mrs. Journoir know about this. The Journoir boys were on a track of cruelty that could one day lead to nothing short of negligent homicide.

"I haven't been praying enough lately," said Buck. "But I sure prayed a lot today."

He surprised me. Buck hadn't told me a lot of his private thoughts in the past, even though he had been kind-hearted and had said things that seemed to hit the nail on the head a lot.

I started thinking about how I had been forgetting to pray more myself, and was letting the 'Haley Roos' of my life cut into my faith and make me do stupid things. Pearl. What must Buck think of me about how I deal with her?

"Buck," I said. "Do you think I'm … well, sort of cold-hearted or something?"

"Cold-hearted? You? Are you kidding? Why would you think that?"

"Because of how I… I get, you know, really annoyed with Pearl sometimes."

"You and the rest of Carson Valley," said Buck. "I have to make myself be nice to her most of the time. But I do because she's sort of an unhappy person."

"I know," I said. "My Mom told me about her. I feel bad that I've disliked her so much, but I just know that if she were to treat me that way again, even knowing more about her, I'd probably just get rip-roaring mad at her all over again!"

"Lissy, you've already been kind to her when she's been pretty awful to you. More than once."

"Thanks, Buck. I…"

"Come in the back with me Lissy. I have something to show you."

We were home. I followed him into the back yard of his Grandfather's house.

"Over here, he said."

We went over to Smokey Blue's corral. Only 'Old Smoke' wasn't alone in there. He was with a white horse with tiny brown flecks on him, and a dark blond mane and tale. He was shorter than Smokey Blue, about the height of Quick. He had a short back and long legs, with a dainty head and large brown eyes.

"What kind of horse is he?" I asked Buck in wonder. He was just the cutest looking horse that I had ever seen - including Nevada, but I would never tell Roger.

"He's an Arab," said Buck. He used to be my Aunt's horse. She's too busy to ride now, and take care of him. I used him a little for cutting, but he's not really built for it. He's a great saddle horse, though, and really good on the trail."

I had got off of Nevada and put my hand over the fence to pet his face and nose.

"He's sure pretty," I said.

"We thought maybe you would want to try him out," said Buck. "My Aunt would like to find a good home for him."

"Me? Really? Wow, I can hardly believe it!"

"If it's not too cold tomorrow, do you want to take him out with me and Quick?"

"Boy, I sure would," I said. "What's his name?"

"Casper," he said. "And Lissy, he isn't fancy, but he's fast," he added, smiling at me.

Buck and I had our heads close together while we studied Casper's face. Buck turned his face to me. My eyes had never been this close to him before. I knew he was thinking about kissing me. I could just tell. I don't know if it was because I was shook up about the missing Roger thing, or not, but I was too nervous to keep my head there for long. A kiss in the future, I thought. I would wait for it.

21

God's Plans

Roger was shook up, but seemed okay after he had got home that night. He told us the whole story of what had happened (to me, about a thousand times) and he was pretty drool-doggy repentant about how he had been talking to Mom lately. His eyes were opened a lot after what he had seen and heard at the Journoirs' and I don't think he was ever quite the same after that. He had a lot of nightmares, we noticed, for a few months, and didn't like gloomy days even more than he had before, but he also was more aware of attitudes in people. Almost like he had made a little mental growth spurt that day.

Roger and I had both learned a lot about ourselves, that early spring, and other people around us. One surprising thing was how God had worked through the most unlikely people, at least to Roger and I, to help us. If it hadn't been for Pearl telling us that she saw Roger talking to Ernie that Sunday morning, we wouldn't have known to talk to him about where Roger went. Also, the carrot that had fallen out of Roger's pocket when

Derek practically turned him upside down, didn't come from our house, but from the refrigerator of Ernie's parents. Even after the atrocious way that Roger had treated Ernie, he had run out a second time that day, to say "Hi" to Roger, and brought the carrot out for Nevada. Roger had said a most ungracious (and he is still repentant to this day for it) "Thanks" to Ernie, stuck it in his back pocket, and rode off. That carrot made us stay and look around there for Roger. It's amazing how God works through the little things in life, the people held in insignificant esteem by certain others, and even through the obnoxious and unlovely.

There was some snow on the ground the next day, but it was sunny, and fairly decent weather for riding, so Buck and I decided to go for a little spin on Quick and Casper. Roger was okay that day, but had the sniffles. Mom said he was probably coming down with a cold, which eventually he did, but he had asked to take Nevada out and go riding with Buck and I. It looked like at first he wouldn't be able to go, but then Dad told Mom that he thought it was important that Roger go with us that day to ride. Sort of to go back out into the world, to remind himself that it wasn't always a bad place, where you were bullied, and didn't have control over your own person, and also, that God has His plans for us, and with Him, we're going to be fine.

The three of us started down the road on our horses. Ernie was by the fence again. Roger saw him. He looked like he was seeing him for the very first time.

Friendly Ernie who sat by him in Sunday School. Red hair, freckles, grinning blue eyes, always ready to share his crayons or scissors with Roger whenever he needed them.

"Lissy, do you think it would be okay to let Ernie ride up here with me on Nevada?"

"Sure you can, Roger. Oh wait! Ask his Dad. He's right there at the mailbox."

His Dad overheard us. "It's okay," he said, and waved his hand at us.

We stopped our horses and Roger said to Ernie, "Hi Ernie! Want a ride! His name is Nevada Sage, but we usually call him "Nevada."

"Good going, Roger Muskrat!" I said to him quietly.

I looked at Buck. He was looking at me in such a strange way. Like he was looking into my soul. It was a serious look, but I had never felt such a warmth from anybody that I had ever met before. "I'd like to shake your hand," he said, as he leaned over from Quick, towards me on Casper.

I kept looking at him, then I said, "Okay," and gave him my hand. We both laughed quietly as he shook it slowly and held on for a minute.

Ernie's face glowed. "Wow! I...I...Wow! Sure!" He bumped his head on the fence as he charged under-neath. But I don't think Ernie even knew that it hurt. Because he was going to ride a real horse - the horse of a boy on his street that he had tried to be friends with for a long time. Now that boy was helping him up on Nevada, showing him how to sit, and how to hold the reins, and was smiling at him with the great kind of smile that one friend gives to another.

The End

Russian Thistle

"I'd like to shake your hand," he said